trihayani

The Untold Story of Draupadi

RUPANDE MEHTA

Readomania

Readomania
An imprint of Kurious Kind Media Private Limited
readomania.com
email: contact@readomania.com
Facebook: facebook.com/iamreadomania
Twitter: twitter.com/iamreadomania
Instagram: iamreadomania

First Published in 2022 by Readomania

ISBN: 978-93-91800-15-4

Typeset in Palatino Linotype by Shine Graphics
Printed and bound in India by Thomson Press India Ltd.

For

Andrew, the love of my life
&
Sophie, the light of my life

Contents

Part I

Draupadi

O Govinda! O resident of Dvārakā! O Kṛṣṇa!
O friend of the gopīs! Do You not know I am being
humiliated by the Kauravas. O Lord! O Lord of Lakṣmī!
O Lord of Vraja! O destroyer of affliction! Save me!
I am drowning in the ocean of the Kauravas!
O Janārdan! O Kṛṣṇa! O Kṛṣṇa! O best of yogīs!
O soul of the world! O origin of the world!
Please protect this surrendered soul, O Govinda!
I am sinking in the midst of the Kurus!

—Draupadi's prayer to Lord Shri Krishna.
Mahābhārata: Sabhā-parva, 67.82–3

I

Krishna sighed and fell to the white sand. The prophecy was coming true. He knew it would, he had even willed it but now that it was here, Krishna was wistful. Two hundred and seventy-five kilometres away, his beloved Dwarka was swallowed by the seas, never to be seen again. Ah, the glamour and splendour it once held! Krishna was sad, no one would ever experience Dwarka in all its pomp and majesty again. Although it would rise seven more times from the ashes, the city would never proclaim its former glory ever again. It would never again be what it was without her one and true *Dwarkadhish*, the only king worthy enough to encapsulate the spirit of a people and claim the title for eternity. Lord Shri Krishna.

Krishna felt nostalgic. He knew these were earthly pleasures that he was bound to leave behind. Krishna struggled though, as he always had to come to terms with the inevitable. His human form was fighting his divinity, wanting more time with those he loved and with those he had come to help. But, alas, his work here was done. The Great War was over, good was reigning over the throne of Hastinapur, and evil had been wiped off from the planet. Only for now though. Krishna knew it was all temporary, for the world would have to battle evil once more very soon.

A sinful age of man was not far away, where destruction would go hand in hand with man's greed and thirst for power. The Kali yuga was closing in on his heels, eager to see Krishna leave so it could dawn, waiting to diminish religion, truthfulness, cleanliness, tolerance, mercy, duration of life, physical strength, and memory in its wake. The worst of all the ages, the Kali yuga, would reward avarice and wrath with humans displaying open hostility and animosity towards each other. Dharma would completely cease to exist with rulers ruling only for their personal benefit, not the welfare of the citizenry until Krishna would have to descend once again, this time in his Kalki form to defeat his arch nemesis, Kali, once and for all.

Krishna could feel Kali's lecherous distant sway, once again feeling the temptation to extend his time and change his destiny. It would be easy for him to do so. He glanced at the hot sun, taking in all the sights around him, melancholy setting in. Krishna would never see his friends again; he would not see any of this again. At least, not in this form or in this yuga. Even in his final moments, he was struggling to reconcile his divinity with his humanity.

Tathaastu. Amen. Krishna had responded to Gandhari when she had cursed his people, the Yadavas.

"I know your true form, O Krishna," Gandhari had said. "I know who you really are. You could have stopped this war, but you did not. I have lost ninety-nine of my children because you preferred bloodshed over diplomacy. I curse you today, O Madhusudan. I curse you that you too shall experience the same agony I did of losing my family, and my clan. Your great and mighty Yadava empire shall one day cease to exist, just like my family has."

Krishna could have argued with Gandhari on the true nature of her sons or their belief in their *adharmi* (godless) cause, but he knew it would lead nowhere. He could have asked her why she had not tried harder to stop her son's greed or curtail her husband's ambitions. He could have asked her so many things...but what good would that do now? For now, it was too late and there was no turning back. Even the Creator could not change what had already come to pass.

A few feet away, the Yadava dynasty was still fighting amongst themselves, drunk, annihilating each other with glee as pre-ordained. In the distance, the orange flag of the mighty Somnath Patan temple blew in the wind. Krishna pensively recalled the last time he was here, helping erect the great temple walls with special sandalwood from Dwarka. Work would continue on the temple, as it always had since Lord Soma first started building it eons ago. Krishna knew Somnath would suffer terribly in the years to come but he also knew it would never fall. Mahadev had blessed it.

"I am always present everywhere but especially in twelve places as the Jyotirlingas. I will be present at Somnath and will protect it, always," Mahadev had said.

Krishna felt the sudden urge to see Somnath's might and wonder one last time. He arose and walked to the temple. Despite the fighting, everything was serene. Everything was quietly waiting to see what he would do next. Krishna walked up the steps of the temple, towards the main hall. The gods were starting to congregate. They were here to witness a divine spectacle. They tailed Krishna as he continued walking towards the *garbhagriha*, the inner sanctum of the temple. Once he reached inside, Krishna stopped and took in the radiance of its energy, the pure power the place emanated. There he closed his eyes and uttered a few words slowly letting them take effect. She would need the protection and the security of the inner sanctum to hold. He needed to hurry but Krishna was in no mood to rush. His older brother, *Dau,* could wait. All of creation could wait. This was important.

After what seemed an eternity, Krishna opened his eyes and slowly walked back out, the Gods spilling behind him. He knew he could no longer prolong the moment. Walking back towards the beach, Krishna descended the steps and sat down on the hot sand, his eyes searching for *Dau,* his older brother Balarama.

Far away in the distance, disgusted with the carnage of brother killing brother, Balarama decided he had enough. Krishna could do whatever he wished. Balarama was done. As he sat down to meditate under a tree, waiting for his divine form to consume him and carry him away from this catastrophic world, Balarama knew he would never return. Between all his earthly lives, Balarama had fulfilled all his roles and all his duties to Krishna. He would not be born among mortals again. At least not until after this *pralaya,* the predestined period of dissolution of the universe.

As the physical world around him started to disappear, a giant *Naga,* the thousand-headed white snake, Ananta, slowly emerged from Balarama's mouth rushing towards the endless ocean, vanishing in its depth. Balarama was gone. Krishna saw *Dau* leave his mortal body and become one with his immortal form, waiting for Krishna to join him once again.

For Krishna, there would be no turning back.

The Yadavas were still fighting. Krishna decided he had seen the spectacle enough. Jara should be along any minute now. The devas started to feel the winds of change. The end was truly near.

Krishna rose from the beach, his emotions conflicted, and slowly started walking towards the forest that lay beside the temple, looking for the chosen tree. Promises had to be fulfilled. After walking for a few minutes, Krishna found her. He bowed, his hands close to his heart and asked for permission to sit down.

"O Goddess, I have come to fulfil my promise," Krishna said, referring to Tilottama's curse from Sage Durvasa who had sent the apsara to Earth in the form of a banyan tree to suffer for an eternity after she inadvertently made the sage wait outside her palace doors. After she conducted severe penance to be freed from Durvasa's curse, Mahadev had granted Tilottama a boon.

"Your travails will end, and you shall re-enter *swargaloka* (heavens) after the Lord in his avatar as Krishna comes to you in his final moments to depart this Earth," Mahadev had blessed.

While Tilottama had waited millennia for this moment, she also knew what it meant. "Oh Lord, I have waited for so long to catch a glimpse of you. And, now you are here. This is a bittersweet moment for me, my Lord. While my salvation awaits, it also means Mother Earth will no longer be your home."

"My time has come, Devi. Mother Earth has her warriors and her protectors. They will fight for her and look after her. My purpose here is done. It is time for me to depart this form," Krishna replied with melancholy.

Hesitatingly, Tilottama obliged. Krishna sat down under her shade, raising his left foot on his right thigh, the same foot injured by Barbarik's arrow. "Barbarik,"

Krishna smiled at the thought of that brave soul who unhesitatingly laid down his life so dharma could win. What a terrible injustice it was but Krishna had learnt that none in the world could match the fearsome power of Barbarik's three arrows, bestowed on him by none other than Mahadev.

"How long would it take for you to finish the Great War, Barbarik?" Krishna had asked Bheema's grandson.

"It would take me one minute, my Lord," came Barbarik's unflinching reply. "One arrow to mark all the targets, second to gather them no matter where they are, and the third to destroy them."

"Show me," Krishna had commanded. Barbarik complied using the leaves of a tree as target practice. Unbeknownst to him, though, Krishna had surreptitiously placed one leaf under his left foot to see what the arrow to mark all targets would do. When Barbarik fired his first arrow, it pierced Krishna's foot to claim the last hiding leaf.

"Be careful, my Lord," Barbarik told Krishna. "Take good care of your foot and never let it be hurt again. My arrow has weakened it. If any sharp object ever hits your foot again, it could lead to your demise."

Seeing the power of his arrows and considering his vow to fight for the weaker side, Krishna made Barbarik realize that he would have to constantly change sides, between the Kauravas and the Pandavas, for the side he was not on would always be more vulnerable. Thus, it would go on until only Barbarik was left alive. Fortunately, Bheema's grandson understood the dilemma, making the decision to end his life, with Krishna granting his final wish. Barbarik's severed head was hoisted upon a tree after receiving the benediction from the Lord himself to witness the Great War.

Krishna sighed at the memory of the incident. His back against Tilottama's mighty trunk, he waited patiently savouring his final moments as many thoughts swirled around his mind.

Moments later, an arrow whizzed by piercing the Lord's foot. Krishna had not taken Barbarik's advice to be careful, in fact, he had willed this moment that would ultimately lead to his departure from this world.

Discovering that his arrow had found no deer but the foot of the Great Lord himself, a disconsolate Jara, rushed towards Krishna. Falling to his feet Jara wailed, "Oh my Lord Madhusudan, I am the most sinful person. I have committed this act out of ignorance. Please forgive my transgression, my Lord." Jara's voice was apologetic and dazed.

Krishna smiled and lovingly put his hand on Jara's head.

"Get up, Jara," he said, affectionately. "You have only done what you were supposed to. It was my desire that this happens. You do not remember this but in another life, you were Vali and I as Ram, used *chhal* (deception) to defeat and kill you. You, Jara, have only done to me what I once did to you. Now, we are even. Go Jara, with my blessing, to the abode of the pious. You have done me great service."

A tearful Jara abidingly touched the Lord's feet, and walked away. His life would never be the same anymore.

Krishna rose from the tree, who now free from her curse headed to *Swarga Loka,* and arrived limping at the holy Triveni Sangam. At Hiran's peaceful banks, his foot throbbing excruciatingly, the Blue Lord performed his final ablutions and worshipped the Lord of all the Worlds, Mahadev. Krishna knew his time had finally arrived. The gods lined up to see this final act of Krishna's life, pouring garlands of fragrant flowers on his earthly body. This birth was truly an enchanted one, even the devas could not help but lament at his end. Krishna had frustrated them, bested them, sometimes even enraged them but in the last moments of his Avatar, they felt nothing but unadulterated love for their Lord. Krishna's divine play, his *Leela,* was truly miraculous!

It was the first day of bright fortnight of Chaitra month when blessing all creatures, the Great Lord closed his eyes preparing to dissolve into the Oneness. As his soul left his mortal body, Krishna saw her face one last time.

Vedavati.

2

Draupadi's eyes opened suddenly. She knew something was wrong. The balance was broken, the equilibrium ruptured but she could not tell what had taken place. A gnawing feeling left her desolate, her heart lurching. Something had happened, she was sure.

Draupadi looked at the sleeping figure of her husband, Yudhishthira. He was snoring softly. Rising from their bed, the queen walked towards the window overlooking the mighty Ganga flowing as ever. It was a resplendent night, the full moon casting shimmering shadows on the flowing water. There were no stars to be seen but the clouds heaved dark, long shadows on the palace grounds. The cool air heralded the arrival of a storm with the wind bellowing at her a message. Something had taken place somewhere but Draupadi could not decipher what the night was trying to tell her. The gnawing feeling in her heart had increased and was now consuming her entire body. She felt the rage of an intense fire threatening to overwhelm her. She knew this familiar feeling, she had felt it several times before and during the Great War. Each time it portended her waxing anxiety, that encompassed the massive urge to fight for her honour and her ill treatment at the hands of the Kauravas.

"What could it be now?" she wondered. Peace had been established throughout all the kingdoms of Hastinapur with Yudhishthira, a wise and just king ruling at the helm. The heathens who had insulted and abused her had met with their rightful end. She could still remember when her invincible Bheema walked in the war tent with the blood of Dushashana in his palms.

"Panchali," he had roared, his mouth oozing. "Here is the blood of the evil Dushashana. Take it and wash your hair with it and complete your oath. That wretch will never be able to touch you or anyone else again."

Draupadi had asked for blood and blood was what she received. When Dushashana dragged her that fateful day, Draupadi had been menstruating. As protocol dictated, she was unable to receive or go to anyone due to her condition. This condition was imposed to allow royal women to rest and recharge their bodies from what was otherwise a very hectic daily life. For Draupadi, this flow of blood also allowed her a respite from the constant fire that raged within her since the day she walked out of the yagna organized by King Drupada of Panchala, as his daughter. By dragging her that day, Dushashana had not only broken royal protocol, but he had also infringed on Draupadi's right to her relief. The flames that arose after that gruesome incident burnt so brightly, they threatened to consume everything and everyone around her. During their exile, Draupadi's fire burned so blazingly, she often ran into the forest at lightning speed, an inferno raging behind her destroying everything. In her search for relief, she consumed many forest animals and once in her rage even tried to kill her husbands—Krishna stopped her—but nothing would help!

Only Dushashana's blood put an end to her torment and soothed her all-consuming fire! The passion and anger she had felt since that day in the Hastinapur assembly when she was disrobed was finally quenched that day in battle. Dushashana was dead and Draupadi and her family were alive. She had finally triumphed! Her insults were finally avenged!

Since that day, Draupadi's anxieties had eased. Krishna had told her they would, though he had also told her they would never dissipate completely. It would always be her pain to bear, this fuming fire that would ebb and flow, filling her with anxiety and pain in one moment and passion and warmth in the next.

Tonight, the flow of her fire signalled her deep pain. The pain that was etched within her soul, that flowed past her conscious and awake mind. This source of pain, Draupadi herself did not recognize for it had been carried forth many times over many lifetimes; none of which Draupadi could remember. But, the deepest parts of her soul did and there it had re-lit itself today, a void that had been left empty despite Draupadi's many subconscious attempts to fill it, hoping for an eventual conclusion.

Draupadi decided it was time to invoke her father. Although a princess of Panchal and daughter to King Drupada, her true father was Agni. The fire that had manifested her time and again, come to her salvation and enabled her to truly rescue herself when she needed it. Although she did not remember why, Draupadi knew Agni was her keeper and supreme protector.

The queen walked out of the bedroom into the quiet palace. The night was eerily silent. Besides the howling wind, no sound was to be heard. Draupadi descended the stairs, walked through the long hallway, making her way past the maids' quarters, entering a large open area. Closing her eyes, she chanted the familiar words to invoke the room.

Two wooden double doors appeared. Draupadi pushed past them and walked inside. The doors closed behind her and the royal queen was lost to the known world.

Inside the empty room, Draupadi walked until she reached its centre. She then sat down and took a deep breath, closed her eyes, and started to meditate.

Ghastly images of bloodshed, carnage, and killing immediately flooded her. She willed herself to go past them. Draupadi saw herself being disrobed, her eyes instantly brimming with tears. She willed herself to go past again. Finally, she reached a place of quiet.

"Om, let me meditate on the great flame, oh, God of fire, grant me with higher intellect, oh, let the radiant God of Fire illuminate my mind," she chanted the Agni Gayatri Mantra softly, each word furthering her resolve.

Outside, time stood still. The earth's rotation stopped, and the river Ganga stopped flowing. Creation waited for Draupadi to come back to the world to resume her activities and assume her role.

Back in the room, Draupadi continued her chanting. Calling out her father to come to her aid with each deep breath, the queen started to reach her innermost being.

Slowly, the dark room began to fill with an orange hue, the light getting brighter with each moment until Lord Agni had finally appeared.

"Open your eyes, my child," Agni, the God of Fire, called out to his daughter.

Draupadi opened her eyes and bowed deeply, paying respects to the Lord.

"What is the cause of your troubles tonight, child? Why have you called me?" Agni asked.

"I cannot tell why, my Lord, but tonight I feel a familiar rage the likes of which I have not felt since we left

Kurukshetra," Draupadi said, referring to the battlefield where the Great War had been fought. "Why do I feel this way, Father? What has happened tonight that I must know? Please grant me this knowledge, Father, so I may feel calm," Draupadi told Agni.

Agni sighed. He knew the reason for Draupadi's troubles, he knew what had transpired that made his daughter feel this way tonight, but he also knew now was not the time for him to deliver the news. He was not the messenger.

"Return to the palace, my dear child," he told the queen. "Even though your heart feels heavy, try and go back to sleep. Everything will be clear in the morning," saying this Agni disappeared, the room turning dark once again.

Draupadi exhaled, her frustration setting in. She had hoped to learn more, but nature had other plans. She got up and headed back to the palace as Agni had instructed. She had no choice but to wait until morning.

The royal messenger hurried along the long and circuitous corridor on his way to the king's chambers. His quick footsteps denoted an urgency the soldiers guarding the halls had frequently seen. The royal messenger, however, was not bringing a usual message. He knew the implications of what he was about to tell the king. The world would never be the same again for anyone, least of all for the brave Pandavas.

King Yudhishthira was sitting in his inner chambers with his queen, Draupadi, when the guard announced the arrival of the royal messenger from Dwarka.

Excited to hear from his dear friend, Yudhishthira arose and made his way to the outer chamber. After a restless night, Draupadi followed close behind, eager to hear what Agni had told her would be divulged this morning. She hoped the royal messenger had her answer.

"Welcome, Bhadra," Yudhishthira greeted the royal messenger. "We are excited about your arrival and cannot wait to hear your message. What news of our dear friend, Krishna?" the king asked.

Bhadra stood with his head lowered to the ground, his eyes downcast, his hands folded. He looked like he was in mourning.

"What ails you, Bhadra?" a panicked Draupadi asked. "You do not look yourself. Are you quite well?"

"Maharaj Yudhishthira, Maharani Draupadi," Bhadra began. "I do not bring good news."

Draupadi felt her stomach lurch. The familiar feeling from the night before was beginning to return.

"What news do you bring?" Yudhishthira asked, eagerly.

"Maharaj, I bring the most solemn news from your friend, our Lord Shri Krishna."

Draupadi waited with bated breath for Bhadra to speak.

"The city of Dwarka has been completely annihilated and swallowed by the sea, O Great King! The entire Yadava dynasty has destroyed each other! What's more, my Lord Madhusudan is no longer among us mortals!" Bhadra said with tears in his eyes.

Draupadi fell to the floor, aghast. She could not believe her own ears. She was on fire once again, the rage commencing in her stomach and spreading through her entire being. Draupadi closed her eyes and took deep gasps of air in.

"Krishna, Krishna, Krishna," she repeated. "You are my being. How can I live in this world if you have chosen to forsake it?"

Meanwhile, Yudhishthira had collapsed on a nearby chair, his head in his hands, unable to believe the words in Bhadra's message. His dear friend, adviser, counsellor, and fiercest advocate was gone. How would he be able to live anymore in a world devoid of Krishna and his divine play? Yudhishthira was speechless.

Bhadra continued, "The Lord knew the inevitable fate that would befall our beloved Dwarka, so he asked me to leave before the seas started to rage inward. While I was leaving he told me, 'Dear Bhadra, you and I will never see each other again in this lifetime. Once Dwarka goes, so will I. You are the sole representative of our dynasty in this world. Once you deliver this message to Yudhishthira and the Pandavas, you are free from the shackles of this world. Go forth in peace after, my friend. You will always have my blessing.'

I saw the sea come inland and I saw Dwarka disappear from the horizon, O King," said Bhadra, wiping hot tears running down his cheeks. "I did not see the Yadavas fighting each other but I have no doubt what the Lord told me has come to pass. I know He is no longer among us for I cannot feel his presence anymore."

Draupadi realized she could not feel Krishna's presence anymore either.

The chamber was silent. Except Draupadi's soft humming, there was no sound to be heard. Bhadra stood in the royal couple's presence for a few more minutes, then retraced his steps back to the outside. Where he would go next, he did not know. This world did not hold much meaning for him. This world did not hold much meaning for anybody.

Inside the palace, Draupadi continued her soft humming calling out to Krishna, angry with him for leaving her behind. She now knew what the world was trying to tell her the night before, what the fire was trying to convey to her. She felt Krishna's presence dim, with it her own essence starting to blur. She never thought Krishna would leave without ever seeing her first. They had made a pact! How could he break it and leave on his own? Krishna knew what she felt and how she lived, how could he leave her behind to deal with the pain and the anguish on her own? What was Draupadi to do now?

Draupadi had five husbands but in this moment none of them could help her extinguish the fire that threatened to consume everything in its path. She knew and understood the terrible anguish her husbands felt. In losing Krishna, they had all lost the most valuable part of themselves, however, in this minute their pain and anguish meant nothing to the queen. For if she did not figure out a way to douse the flames raging within her, nothing would be left behind.

Draupadi knew she had to do something quick.

The queen left the palace hurriedly, arriving at the banks of the river Ganga. Intending to invoke the Goddess, Draupadi sat deep in prayer on the waterfront.

"Hear my plea, O Mother Goddess. Please come to me," the queen cried out repeatedly.

One of the most sacred and revered goddesses of all the rivers, Mother Ganga, wearing a golden crown, dazzling in white, holding a water lily and a flute in her two back hands, rosary in the front left hand and right hand in blessing mode, appeared before Draupadi. She shone with the splendour of a thousand suns, effulgent with poise, grace, and benevolence.

"What can I do for you, O mighty queen? You have the entire world underneath your feet, yet you have chosen to call me. How can I be of service to you, Maharani Draupadi?" the river Goddess asked.

"This world no longer means anything to me, O Goddess," the queen grieved. "The light of my heart is gone. Krishna has abandoned us and left this Earth," Draupadi said.

"Yes, Shri Krishna is no longer in the mortal world. But, do not despair, for you know the Lord is transcendental and lives across time. He will never forget those who worship him and carry his image in their heart," the Goddess said.

"But, he has forgotten me, O Goddess," Draupadi quailed. "He promised never to leave me alone on this Earth, always walk alongside me and help me soothe the fire that burns within me. What am I to do now? How am I to quell this raging beast? I am afraid, O Goddess. I am afraid that this fire will burn ever so brightly destroying everything Krishna and my husbands fought for. I fear for them. I fear for everyone. Help me, O Goddess. Tell me what to do," saying this Draupadi burst into tears.

"The Lord has never left you nor will he ever leave you, O queen! You of all people should know that but perhaps you do not remember. Let me tell you who you really are, Panchali. You have been called many names in this lifetime—Draupadi, Krishnaa, Panchali, Yajnaseni—but you have always remained the prime epitome of divine strength and power in this world. You, the most dynamic of women know what to do. Yet, if you need my help, go to the temple of Somnath Patan, where all will be revealed to you. Go seek the Lord's word there and all will be clear to you."

Goddess Ganga then vanished leaving a relieved Draupadi on the banks.

It was time to visit Somnath Patan. Draupadi would set off first thing the following morning.

Maharani Draupadi stood at the foot of the majestic Somnath Patan temple, the fire raging within her. It was a bright, cloudless day. A gentle breeze blew, wafting the surroundings with the honeyed smell of Passion flowers (Krishna Kamal), Arabian Jasmine (Mogra), and Night Blooming Jasmine (Raat Rani) flowers that grew in abundance. Birds flitted from tree to tree tweeting the sweet arrival of spring. Indeed, some trees showed bountiful buds with new life looking to leap forth. Even from where she stood, the queen could hear the roar of the waves, buzzing with their dormant strength, as they crashed gently on the shore.

The queen took in the grandeur of the temple. An open hallway with terraced steps of Kanjur stone on both sides led up to the sea, with a retaining seawall on the south to prevent the waves from crashing in. Elaborate classical architecture and extravagant sculptures of apsaras and deities adorned the temple walls on the outside. The Eastern façade welcomed visitors with a giant stone carving of Suryanarayana, the destroyer of darkness, while the Western side was greeted by Madhava Deva. Devi Bhavani, seated on her tiger, bedecked the Northern wall while the raging seas to the South carried the Badabagni deep into the ocean.

Approximately sixty-five kilometres wide and long, the temple was situated between the plains of two rivers—Vajrini in the East, and Nyankumati in the West. Known by many different names over many *kalpas* (aeons), Somnath as it was called in the seventh *kalpa*, was always sacrosanct and protected by Lord Ganesha, the remover of obstacles.

Draupadi, aware of her consecrated surroundings, inched closer to the temple. Outwardly, it seemed like just another ordinary day. Everything was doing what it was supposed to. The village, nearby, would be bustling with the humdrum of everyday life unaware of Draupadi's presence here or the anxieties that plagued her mind.

As the queen approached the temple, she detected the creamy, exotic smell of sandalwood, especially brought from Dwarka for its distinct warmth and earthiness. Dwarka's memory brought a brief smile to her lips, instantly replaced by the horror she felt of its eventual demise. Draupadi took some solace in knowing it was all part of Krishna's plan. Draupadi standing here was also part of Krishna's plan. She would trust it all as she trusted him.

Draupadi started to climb the steps of the temple with Krishna on her mind. With each step, she knew she was coming closer to her beloved, her Lord, the only one who truly understood the pain and the agony she was dealing with.

"Krishna, Krishna," she chanted, as she drew closer and closer to the temple. Draupadi had almost made it to the outer part of the temple courtyard when she suddenly stopped climbing. The queen swung around feeling an eerie presence behind her. She could see no one. From where she stood, Draupadi could clearly see the garden adjoining the temple walls on either side with the four pillars erected to mark each direction. From here, the ocean sounded even more menacing, Draupadi could see the undulating waves as they formed and crested on the pearly white sand, gleaming under the shining sun. She stood there a second more, imagining a massive tidal wave coming inward towards her and shuddered at the mere thought. "Poor Dwarka," she thought once more lamenting the sinking of the city of gold.

The queen's piercing hazel eyes searched in the distance to find the source of her distraction. Far off, she could see the forest lining with thick banyan, peepal, and neem trees. Unable to reconcile the interruption, without a second thought, Draupadi hastily descended the temple steps and made her way towards the forest.

As if in a trance, Draupadi walked the forest floor hurriedly looking for something she did not quite know. Her mind struggling to keep pace with her feet, Draupadi's eyes nervously glanced around to recognize any threats. The Gir forest, whose borders were not too far away, harboured countless dangerous animals. Without a weapon or anyone to protect her, the queen would not be safe.

In the middle of the forest, Draupadi came upon a large expanse of clear land. "This is very unusual," she thought to herself. Bending down on the ground, she could see the remnants of a banyan tree that stood there not too long ago. "What happened here?" she wondered, gazing at the land where only a few days ago Jara's arrow had landed the ultimate blow on Krishna's foot.

Draupadi continued walking but the thick forest was now clearing out. The trees and vegetation grew less dense, and the queen could sense the presence of water. Draupadi heard cries of seagulls in search of food and realized she had walked the trail towards the holy Triveni of Hiran, Kapila, and Sarasvati rivers.

Bowing her head deeply, Draupadi paid obeisance to the holy confluence. Nearing the banks, the queen saw a bright yellow scarf at its mouth. She instinctively knew. Draupadi grabbed the scarf in her hands, kneeling in the wet mud, swaying in the realization that she had found Krishna.

"Krishna, Krishna," she started chanting again. "My Lord, tell me why have you brought me here today? What can I do? Show me the way, O Madhusudan, O Keshav. Show me the path I need to walk. Help me, my Lord. Do not abandon me in time of my desperate need."

The mud on her face, mixed with the tears streaking down her cheeks but Draupadi did not care. For she had received all she had asked for. The Lord had heard her prayer and left her with a way to return to her. Draupadi was overjoyed.

"O, Maharani Draupadi," a female voice called out to her. Draupadi looked up startled.

"You are the Lord's most beloved, his sister, his friend, his confidant. Without you, this birth would have been exceedingly difficult to bear. Your presence and your company were a joy for him to behold. The Lord would never abandon you. Alas, the Lord cannot take you away yet as more needs to be done," the voice said.

Wiping her tears, Draupadi stood up. Unable to seek the source of the voice, she assumed it was a divine presence.

She folded her hands again and said, "O, divine one, I am blessed that the Lord has sent you here. Without his presence, this world holds no meaning for me. However, you say there is more to be done. What more must I do? The world has been freed from the evil of the Kauravas. That wicked Dushashana is dead and with his demise my insult has been avenged. Yudhishthira sits on the throne of Hastinapur ruling with compassion and mercy. What more does the Lord command to be done? I pray this is only his *Leela* for if it is not, I may not be able to bear it any longer."

"Freedom is your right, Maharani, but you may not attain it yet. I have called you here, the place the Lord chose to give up his earthly body and ascend to his transcendental form, for a purpose. Fulfil all your tasks and you will be united unto the Supreme Being," the voice continued.

"I shall do whatever you command, O divinity," Draupadi answered.

And, so, the voice began.

"Long ago, during a long battle between the Devas and the Asuras, Lord Vishnu went against dharma and killed Sage Bhrighu's wife, who was unfairly protecting the Asuras, with his Sudarshan Chakra. When the sage found out, he cursed the Lord saying the Lord would be born in human form many times and suffer the pain of death. Our Lord's last form was a result of this curse. Sage Bhrigu also stipulated that the Lord would be unable to achieve his true transcendental form, after each birth, until Mother Kali visits and blesses his mortal coils. You, Maharani, are an incarnate of Goddess Kali. Without your blessing, the Lord cannot completely attain his divinity.

Draupadi was stunned. "I am an incarnate of Goddess Kali?"

"You indeed are. You could have destroyed all the Kauravas and the Pandavas with a single thought. The Lord did not give you this knowledge because the war served a greater purpose, a way to convey to the future that evil is never rewarded, and dharma always wins over adharma. He would not have been able to preach his Bhagavad Gita without this war which clearly enunciates, 'The side on which the Lord is, is the side that always wins'," the voice explained.

"You remember the time during your period of exile when you wanted to avenge your insults by killing one of your husbands?" the voice asked.

"Yes," replied Draupadi, rather sheepishly. "The fire raged through me, I was unable to think of anything else but my revenge and the inability of my husbands who stood there like pillars instead of protecting me."

"The Lord knew, and the Lord stopped you," the voice clarified. "Now that you know, know this too—we cannot tarry any longer. Arjuna will be on his way soon."

"Arjuna is on his way here? Why is he coming here?" Draupadi asked.

"The Lord has summoned Arjuna to come and perform his final rites. Mortals believe without completion of the final rites; the Lord's soul cannot rest. They do not understand that the Lord is above all of that but since they will insist and not believe that the Lord has indeed departed Earth, the Lord bade Arjuna and some chosen villagers so the rites can be completed and witnessed. This way there shall be no doubt left in anyone's mind that the Lord is no longer on Earth."

"O divine presence, I do not doubt your words but how do you know what the Lord wishes?" the queen asked.

"I know because the Lord blessed me to know. As you are about to achieve your purpose, in this place, this is one of mine. The Lord enabled me to carry this task out and make sure it was fulfilled. So, Maharani, let us proceed. The Lord's mortal coils are under the neem tree by the river's mouth."

Draupadi ran on to the river's edge. There she saw her beloved Krishna, sitting peacefully, with his eyes closed under the tree. He looked calm and serene as if he were in a deep sleep. His face conveyed harmony and although his soul was no longer there, his blue-skinned body glowed with a deep rich hue.

Draupadi rushed towards him, kissing his feet, her tears falling unrestrained. "Krishna, Krishna, Krishna," she began chanting again.

"Maharani," the voice called out.

"Please," Draupadi said, wailing. "Let me take in this image of my Lord one last time. Please, do not rush me."

"Maharani, I know how you feel. The entire universe feels the same way. While we all understand your pain, there is an urgency to this task so we must hurry."

But, Draupadi could not move. She was transfixed at the spot of Krishna's feet. How could she let go of her best friend, her confidant, her protector, the deepest love she had ever known? As she wept, Draupadi could hear Krishna's last words, "O *sakhi,* my dearest friend, you are the pre-eminence to womanhood in this world. Without your force, the fight against injustice could never have been won. Do not lament over your losses or worry about the raging fire within you for soon you shall be reprieved."

How Draupadi wished she could hear Krishna's voice again, feel his touch and delight in his company.

Her friend sitting calmly before her, who could be napping, would never speak, touch, or visit her again. The realization brought fresh tears to the queen's eyes as she started sobbing once more.

"O queen. Please, let us make haste," the voice spoke again.

Her heart aching with the magnitude of her loss, Draupadi stood up unsteadily, wiping her tears, trying to compose herself. She still held Krishna's yellow scarf in her hands. Instinctively, the queen knew exactly what to say and before she could comprehend, the words flowed out of her mouth.

Thus, Draupadi, the queen of Hastinapur, wife of the mighty Pandavas, daughter of King Drupada, princess of Panchal stood over Shri Krishna's mortal coils and blessed him.

"Be blessed, O Krishna. While your human birth was a sacred period for this earth, the time has come for you to depart. I, Draupadi, free you from the entirety of this birth. Make your way towards Vaikuntha and be united with your Divine Form, O Vishnu."

The entire cosmos took a collective sigh of relief. Vishnu was free, at last.

The voice spoke again. "Blessed are you, O Maharani, for you have freed the Lord. The known and the unknown world will never forget your deed here today. Now, it is time for you to return to the temple for your task here is complete."

"What happens at the temple, O divinity?" Draupadi asked.

"That is for you to find out. It is your destiny alone, Maharani. But, before you go, please enter the holy waters here at the Triveni so you may be blessed."

"I shall do that, but pray tell me its purpose," said Draupadi.

"When the Lord chose this spot to give up his earthly body, the Triveni of Hiran, Kapila, and Sarasvati was blessed with his divine effervescence. His blessing now enables anyone who enters the river at this precise spot to be reunited with him. That person shall be freed from the endless cycle of birth and death and achieve moksha."

Draupadi bowed in prayer, grateful for this heavenly knowledge.

"Before I leave, O divine one, would you be so kind as to show me your human form?" she asked.

In a flash of piercing light, Goddess Sarasvati appeared before Draupadi in her complete form. Dazzling in a white sari with golden borders, the Goddess epitomized purity holding a garland and a book in two arms, while her two front arms gently played the veena. A soft smile on her lips, the Goddess had kindness in her eyes and a maternal generosity. True to her nature, Mother Sarasvati exemplified wisdom and poise.

Draupadi was stunned. She touched the golden feet of the Goddess and asked for her blessing.

"Ask for a boon, Maharani. What would you like?" Mother Sarasvati told the queen.

"I do not ask anything for myself, O Mother," said Draupadi. "I, however, wish that my children and the Kuru line is safe and reigns for a long time. As you know we have suffered great loss during and after the war," the queen said referring to the murder of her five sons, the Upapandavas, by Ashwatthama. "The Kuru line rests only on Abhimanyu's son, Parikshit. Protect him and make sure he never has to fight the way we had to," Draupadi replied.

"Maharani, you have nothing to worry about. The Great War will never be fought again. None of the three worlds would be able to bear the burden. But, as far as your line is concerned, I bless the Kurus with a long and harmonious reign. Abhimanyu's son, Parikshit, will have many sons who will conquer new territories and spread goodwill on this earth. Even after two thousand years, the Kurus will still be rulers, and your line will be remembered by humankind for eternity. Be assured, Maharani.

But, it is you who will be glorified in history. Your sacrifice, your penance, and your atonement will serve as an example for all of humankind to follow. You will be exemplified as the virtuous queen who always fought for what she believed in and never once gave up the fight for what is right. It is you who will serve as an example of a fierce woman who never accepted her fate and was never afraid to challenge the status quo. You, Maharani, will be greater and stand higher than the achievements of all your husbands. History will never forget you, O great queen."

Draupadi bowed to Goddess Sarasvati who blessed her and vanished.

Content, the queen dipped at the confluence, exalting in its holiness. She then started to make her way back to the temple and to the surprises that awaited her there.

Draupadi entered the base of the Somnath temple making her way into the pavilion, smelling the exotic sandalwood that lined the walls. Besides the soft jingle of her tinkling anklet bells, the place was quiet. She walked through the antechamber, glittering with dazzling precious gemstones and jewels, that lay between the mandap and the holy inner sanctum. Half-mindedly, Draupadi glanced at the watercolour paintings that decked the ceiling illuminating the entire arena with a glistening hue. The omnipresence of the temple was otherworldly and overflowed through her.

Draupadi then walked into the holiest of the holy places, the *garbhagriha,* inner sanctum and noticed it was dark with a radiant energy vibrating through its midst; unlike anything she had ever experienced. Crowned by the fifteen-metre-high peak, the inner sanctum sat directly underneath, forming the main vertical axis of the temple with the two together representing the axis of the world through Mount Kailash. The most famous of all Shiv *jyotirlingas,* the shrine of Lord Shiva, the *Swayambhu* Somnath Linga that had manifested on its own, sat in the centre, radiating the brilliance of the Sun, the heat of *Agni* (fire) and a sacred mix of desire, knowledge, and devotion.

Draupadi felt nonplussed. The day had so far had left her reeling. She could not decipher her feelings or understand why she was sitting here in the *garbhagriha*. All she knew was that she needed answers, not just to quieten the raging fire within her but also to understand its source and reason. Draupadi needed to understand much more than her birth, but her mind spun at the implications of such an inquiry. Goddess Sarasvati had called her an incarnate of Mother Kali. Draupadi could have avenged her insults and ended the war by killing everyone with a single thought. What did all this mean and why was this being divulged to her now, after Krishna had departed? Draupadi knew she would not feel at peace until it was all revealed. Her answers lay in this chamber, but she was not sure where or how to extricate them.

Prostrating at the *jyotirlinga,* Draupadi offered the Supreme God of destruction her obeisance and thus spoke, "O Mahadev, you are the supreme god of all gods. Nothing is a secret from you. You well know the purpose of my visit to Somnath today. While I do not claim to understand the mysteries of this universe, I wish you to show me the path so I may free myself from this torment. Please help me calm this raging fire and free my troubled soul." Draupadi then sat down cross legged, closed her eyes, and started meditating. She did not intend to get up until it was all revealed.

Sitting in intense prayer, Draupadi meditated until day turned into night. When morning came, Draupadi was still seated in her devout fervour. So, she sat, until several days and several nights passed.

Outside, the world started to change; spring turned to summer, with trees in full bloom, butterflies fluttering, and young birds starting to take flight. Inside the inner sanctum, time stood still where nothing changed except Draupadi's appearance which was starting to wear. The queen's powerful *siddhi* (paranormal power) carried her instinctive mind and her physical body to the *nakshatriya kshetra,* the realm of the stars, where no mortal being could hinder her worship.

Thus, even though the daily bustle of the temple's activities continued unabated—visitors came and went; priests performed their services and the devadasis entertained throngs of guests—no one could disturb Draupadi's deep penance.

With each passing day, Draupadi's penance intensified, and her power increased. Fearing her rage and the fire that burnt through her would destroy the known universe, the *Nakshatra Devas* (star gods) approached Mahadev.

"O mighty Lord, Maharani Draupadi sits at the *jyotirlinga* in Somnath. While we do not know what she wants, her intense penance has made us all very afraid," Bharani, a star god, prayed to Mahadev.

"What do you fear, O Lord? You are a mighty God while she is just a Maharani," Mahadev toyed with them.

"We know she is not *just* a Maharani, O Mahadev," Mrigashira said. "Maharani Draupadi is an incarnate of Mother Kali and if continues her meditation uninterrupted, the fire that rages through her will destroy everything."

"We have all come here today to implore you to visit Maharani Draupadi and fulfil her heart's desire, O Pashupatinath. We are sure you know what she desires," Ashwini said. "With each passing day, she gets stronger and the fire within her burns brighter. Please visit her, Lord and save us all."

Mahadev smiled. He knew all about Draupadi's discipline.

"Maharani Draupadi's intense penance has reached me," Mahadev responded. I know what her heart desires. Worry not, O *devas*, her fire will not destroy anyone for I shall visit her and soothe her enraged spirit. Now return to your *lokas* unhindered and be at peace. Maharani Draupadi is my responsibility."

The gods bowed to Mahadev and satisfied with his response returned to their abodes knowing they had nothing to worry about. Very soon, the world would be safe from the great queen's raging fire.

Mahadev knew the breath-taking power and astounding strength of the queen's fire. He had come face to face with it many times before. He had suffered tremendous loss because of this fire. Mahadev realized the time had come. The queen needed answers and nothing short of that would satisfy her. He knew her nature and knew she would never give up. To avoid any further damage, Mahadev would have to visit her soon.

Leaving his abode in Mount Kailash, Mahadev headed to Somnath, the seat of the *Tatvamaya Kshetra,* known so for comprising all the primal elements of the Holy Trinity—Brahma, Vishnu, and Mahesh.

Inside the temple, the radiant energy emanating from the *garbhagriha* was replaced by the intensity of a heat only matched by the queen's penance. Draupadi sat in front of the *jyotirlinga,* continuing her deep search for answers. Her clothes looked worn, and her hair was matted. Without food or drink, the queen had been sitting there for one hundred days and one hundred nights with only one goal in mind. With each breath the force of her fire grew, encapsulating ever so slightly more and more of the universe.

Slowly, a dim blue light started to emerge in the chamber. Growing ever so gradually, the light spread throughout the *garbhagriha,* cooling the inner chamber. Despite a considerable drop in temperature, the queen continued unabated until Mahadev in all his glory appeared and called her out.

"O, Maharani Draupadi. Open your eyes. Your intense self-discipline has reached me for I have arrived. Open your eyes, O great queen. Your penance is successful."

Hearing his voice and sensing his presence, the queen finally stopped her chanting and opened her eyes. Her vision, blurry at first, took a few moments to adjust before she saw Mahadev in his grandeur standing before her.

His blue body in tiger skin, Mahadev looked glorious with a crescent moon in his matted hair and a snake around his neck. While the Neelkanth's throat glowed with the trapped *Halahala* (poison), his third eye was covered with three lines of sacred ash, representing his all-pervading nature, his superhuman power and intense spiritual wealth. His left hand holding the *dumroo* (a small, two-headed drum), Mahadev's right hand was stretched out in the blessing gesture. The Lord's eyes filled with love and compassion, Mahadev oozed magnificence with every fibre of his being.

Draupadi bowed deeply taking in the majestic sight that stood before her. Her hands in prayer position, her eyes filled with devotional tears, the queen sighed repeatedly unable to say anything.

"Tell me, Maharani," Mahadev said. "Why have you called me? What would you like me to do for you?"

But, the queen befuddled by the intensity of her penance and the sight that stood before her, could not utter a single word. Mahadev smiled. Draupadi would need some help. Slowly and cautiously, the Gangadhara loosened a strand of his hair, releasing an urgent fountain of water that surged upward through his tresses, descending on Draupadi's dry and malnourished lips. The famished queen drank the holy Ganga with deep gratification.

Her body now feeling satiated and sustained, the queen found the energy for her words.

"Mahadev, truly I am blessed for having seen you in this magnificent form. My life is complete with just this moment; however, I know I have more to do. I have been requesting your presence to understand the purpose of my life," Draupadi replied.

"Is there anything specific you wish to understand, Maharani?" Mahadev asked her mischievously.

Draupadi sighed again.

"Mahadev, nothing is hidden from you. You are the source of all knowledge and the destroyer of all things. Your power in this cosmos is unsurpassed and without beginning or end. You are the Great Dissolver; the end of all things and the Great Creator; the primordial being existing before the beginning of time. Nothing is ever a secret to you, my Lord. You know more than I can ever imagine and know that I am looking for respite from this raging fire within me. If I am not relieved, I do not know what it will do. I am very afraid, O Rudra. Help me douse this indomitable inferno that seethes my mind, body, and soul."

"You are wise to be concerned, Maharani, however, there is no reason to be afraid. You are so much more than you know and remember. Your power is absolute and although you possess the ability to destruct everything, your empathy is great. You do not remember who you are. So, let me tell you."

And so, began Mahadev reminding the queen of her true form.

"You are *kala shakti,* the power of time. It is within you that this universe finds the eventual truth: the impermanence of all things.

The ultimate power of time that carries us all from death to immortality resides within you. It is within you that we find the boundless space and the limitless void.

You are the holder of the *vidyut shakti,* the lightning force of consciousness that is the supreme power. Without your power, creation would not exist.

Your *kriya shakti* is the power of conversion at play behind the transformation of life. It is the energy of creation and inspiration.

You are the manifestation of cosmic wisdom that Arjuna sought at Kurukshetra and Lord Shri Krishna narrated in the Gita. You are the supreme power of all beings; great and small.

It was you who appeared to the Pandava soldiers in their dreams and entered the battle at Kurukshetra amidst an attack by Ashwatthama. You drank the blood of the lawless kings to rid the earth of her burden.

The power of creation and the sheer force of nature exist within you.

You are the inner power of *yoga shakti,* the energy in flow with the universe; the *nirodhi shakti,* the great restraining power; the power of *neti-neti,* not this nor that, which helps negate everything that is not the *Atman,* the soul.

Kundalini, the secret power of transformation within every being, resides within you.

You are *Bhavatarini,* the redeemer of the universe, liberator of her devotees from the ocean of *samsara,* the circle of repeated birth and death due to karma.

The primordial energy-consciousness-bliss, you are the *Mahamaya* who creates the universe and liberates the soul from the clutches of *Maya,* this illusion that exists all around humans.

You show the universe the Divine life and joy that manifests out of absolute stillness and transcendence.

You are the symbol of Mother Nature herself, her preserver; primordial, creative, nurturing, loving, and benevolent.

The creator of the Vedas, you are the slayer of human ego and the revealer of divine knowledge.

Nirgun, pure and beyond the touch of *Maya,* the illusion that exists around humans, you exist forever and through time.

You are formless, limitless, boundless, yet you exist in every form and every essence of this universe. Without you nothing could form, bind, or hold itself.

You existed in the *Hiranyagarbha,* the golden primordial egg, yet you are its Mother.

You have always existed and will always exist, untouched by the rules of *sanskriti* (culture) and *pitrutantra* (patriarchy). You emerged from Agni in the Dwapara Yuga, to assist Shri Krishna and the Pandavas re-establish law on this earth.

You are *Brahman,* the Ultimate Reality of the universe in its supreme and unmanifest state.

You are everything to this universe and to me, you are my consort. Without you, *kala* (time) is powerless and cannot exist. Without you, I am nothing.

Know your true form, O queen, for you are so much more than you think."

Draupadi stood in shocked silence contemplating the intensity of Mahadev's words. She believed his words for how could he ever deceive her but struggled to truly accept their meaning. How could she, daughter of the King of Panchal, wife to the brave Pandavas, friend to Shri Krishna, be all those things Mahadev had described? Her soul struggled within the bounds of her human existence to fathom the possibilities of what it all actually meant. And, above all, how was all of this supposed to help quench her fire?

Mahadev saw doubt and uncertainty etched on the queen's face. He smiled kindly. He understood her limitations and knew a way to help her reconcile her doubts.

"O Maharani," he began again. "I see doubt on your face and in your eyes. You believe my words yet struggle with their meaning. It is not you but the limitation of you, in this human form that cannot really understand the reality of my words. For your soul is boundless but wrapped in this human body, *Maya,* the illusion that exists around humans has trapped your mind in its grasp. Until you are free from it, I am afraid nothing can help you."

Draupadi languished at Mahadev's words.

"I do not know what to do, O Lord. For I trust the words you speak to me are the truth, but my mind is spinning at its allusions. I hear your words and I understand them, yet, I cannot completely realize them. Your words make me giddy with fear. How can I be all those things yet not know any of it? How can I be the keeper of the universe yet not feel a thing?

I do not remember going to the battlefield at Kurukshetra, my Lord. I do not ever remember fighting Ashwatthama or drinking any *adharmi* (godless) kings' blood. I would not forget that even for a mere second for that blood would have helped me calm my fire. I believe every word you say, O Shiv Shambhu, but how can I be something I know I am not?"

The queen's shoulders dropped, and she cradled her head in her hands. Mahadev could tell it was all proving extremely difficult for her to accept.

"I am also not sure, O Maheshwar, how this knowledge will help me calm my fire. I do not intend any disrespect, but it seems I may have to find another way to quell myself." The queen looked resigned and defeated.

"You of all people accept defeat so quickly?" Mahadev asked. "I expected more from you," the Lord teased the queen.

"What would you have me do, O Neelkanth?" Draupadi asked. "You say it's the limitation of me, in this human form that cannot actually understand the reality of your words. This means the only way I can understand the reality of what you say is when I discard this human form. And, I am afraid this fire within me, if not quenched soon, will annihilate everything before I discard this human form."

"You say you do not feel or remember anything yet the fire within you will annihilate everything. How do you feel or remember this fire, O Maharani?" Mahadev asked.

"I do not remember the source or the reason of this fire. I only remember always feeling it within me. I know Lord Agni is my true father for I emerged from him when my adopted father, the king of Panchal, performed his yagna," the queen explained. "I do not remember anything prior to that. Who I was or what I felt? I do not know."

"No, you would not, Maharani. Loss of those memories is the price you paid when you took the form of Draupadi, the daughter of the king of Panchal and wife to the Pandavas. You do not remember but I know. You feel this all-consuming fire about you because you have always emerged from and entered back into the fire. The fire has been your primogenitor and your demolisher for eons. Lord Agni has been your father every time you have taken human form but you in your divine form surpass all of Agni's power and might."

"How many times have I been born on earth, O Lord?" the queen inquired.

"Prior to your birth as Panchali, you have come to earth three other times. In Satya yuga, you were Vedavati, the knower of the Vedas.

In Treta yuga, you emerged from the fire, as Sita's Chaya, when Lord Vishnu took human form as Shri Rama to kill King Ravana and in the Dwapara yuga, you were born twice.

Once as Nalayani, the daughter of Nala, the king of Nishadha kingdom and Damayanti, his queen the princess of Vidharba, upon a boon from Lord Agni. In that birth, you married Sage Mugdala, and together both of you became ancestors to your adopted father in this life, King Drupada in whose home you took your second birth of the Dwapara yuga, after emerging from the fire.

Because you were born in each of the yugas, you Draupadi, are also called *Trihayani*; one who appears in all the three ages."

Draupadi felt calm. The fire still blazing did not feel as extreme anymore. The knowledge Mahadev gave her so far was helping quench her thirst.

"I have so many questions, Pashupatinath," Draupadi said.

"I know you do. And, I am here to answer them. In reality, your fire will not die down until all your questions are answered," Mahadev pre-empted the queen.

"What must I do then, O Lord?" A confused Draupadi asked.

"I know what you must do. But, instead of telling you, I will show it to you. However, before we begin, remember, O queen, the path you are about to walk on can be treacherous and will demand a lot out of you. Are you indeed sure you are ready and able to do this?" Mahadev asked.

Draupadi felt a slight hesitation. She knew she had to travel this path to liberate herself but now faced with deciding, the queen felt a part of her holding herself back.

The Lord continued, "The path I am going to take you on will teach you what you need to re-learn and what your soul needs to fulfil its obligations. Your intense duties have spanned across several lifetimes. You have struggled and burned for aeons, throughout all your past lives. The time has finally come for you to seek your salvation, however, the road we take will not be easy. So, think twice before you answer, O queen."

Draupadi had some doubts, but she knew she would always be safe with Mahadev. And, hadn't Mahadev just said she would be liberated with this knowledge? Draupadi decided she would walk the path. Despite all the recent revelations of her glory, the queen could only think of relief. Relief from her inferno. Relief from her rage. Knowing that Mahadev would help her finally meant Draupadi would get the answers she so desperately sought for so long. They would help soothe her, calm her, and ultimately liberate her. Draupadi was ready.

"I am ready, my Lord. I will go seek the answers I need with you," the queen confirmed.

"I am glad to hear of your decision, O queen, but before we go anywhere, we first need to do something.

I need to give you divine vision, the ability to travel and see across time. Your searing eyes are going to see many things they will like and other things they may not. Your responsibility is only to watch. You cannot intrude upon any of the multiple things you will see, neither can you reveal your presence. If you do, the spell will break, and you shall be confined to your suffering for many aeons to come," Mahadev explained.

"I understand everything you say, Shiv Shambhu. I shall not interfere, nor shall I reveal my presence to anyone. But, pray tell me, O Lord, what if they see me without any fault of mine?" the queen asked.

"They shall not have the ability to see you. Only you shall be able to see them. So, the only way for them to know you are present is if you divulge it yourself," Mahadev said.

"I give you my word, my Lord. I shall not divulge myself," said Draupadi her hands folded, and her head bowed.

With her promise, the queen acquiesced to the cardinal rule of time travel.

Mahadev then deftly whisked his fingers, bringing forth a bright golden light that travelled to the queen's forehead. There it planted itself firmly.

"It is done, and you are ready," Mahadev said with finality.

The queen did not feel any different, but she knew she was. As her 'new' eyes looked upon the inner sanctum she had inhabited for so long, they now saw much more. She could see several souls strung across time, withering in pain and anguish. Draupadi saw the hand of the demon Kali and the speed with which he was destroying every known being, including her husbands, in the universe instilling them with avarice and greed. She immediately felt anguish and terribly overwhelmed.

"Do you see more than you bargained for, O queen?" Mahadev asked.

"I see the pain and suffering of humans as well as the source, Pashupatinath. The realization that I am one of them makes me ashamed of my ignorance," the queen replied.

"Yes, humans can be ignorant but do not forget that the purpose of humanity is to seek illumination and enlightenment. Along the way, pain and suffering will always be constant companions for without the presence of night, humans cannot appreciate the importance of sunlight. Even Lord Shri Krishna struggled with his humanity although his knowledge of his divinity was profound and accessible to him. So, do not be embarrassed of what you are and what you have done. You are only achieving the purpose you set out to achieve in this human form."

Draupadi then saw a sight that baffled her. Far away from here, the queen saw herself in her palace at Hastinapur welcoming guests and presiding over a large banquet. Her mind spun. What was she witnessing? She decided to ask Mahadev.

"I also see myself in Hastinapur living my daily life, my Lord. Pray tell me how this is possible, while I am standing here with you? Is that really me from today or is this me from some other time?" the queen asked puzzled.

"Yes, Maharani. That is indeed you today. Your divinity enables you to be in two places at once. So, while your quest for knowledge continues here with me, another part of you will remain at the palace with the Pandavas and will continue performing your daily duties there. One cannot be abandoned for the pursuit of another.

On this journey, you will see a lot more that may seem inexplicable. Know that the rules you live by on Earth, are not the same rules for this universe. A lot you see may capture your attention, lure you and sway your mind. On this route, you may be tempted to abandon course, to give up and forsake your journey. The choice, of course, is always yours. If you choose to be swayed or abandon your course, you may do so.

But, know that once it is done, you can never return. The opportunity that is granted to you, here, today will not be given again until after this *pralaya*. You would be wise to concentrate on only that which is relevant for your current purpose and discard the rest." Mahadev concluded.

Draupadi nodded in acknowledgement. Although a bit uncertain on what was next, the queen understood the circumstances presented to her.

With that, a flash of light appeared that carried the immeasurable, all powerful, deathless Lord Mahadev along with Maharani Draupadi, on a journey across time.

Part II

Vedavati

Then even non-existence was not there, nor existence,
There was no air then, nor the space beyond it.
What covered it? Where was it? In whose keeping?
Was there then cosmic fluid, in depths unfathomed?
Then there was neither death nor immortality
nor was there then the torch of night and day.
The One breathed windlessly and self-sustaining.
There was that One then, and there was no other.
At first there was only darkness wrapped in darkness.
All this was only unilluminated cosmic water.
That One which came to be, enclosed in nothing,
arose at last, born of the power of knowledge.
In the beginning desire descended on it—
that was the primal seed, born of the mind.
The sages who have searched their hearts with wisdom
know that which is, is kin to that which is not.
And they have stretched their cord across the void,
and know what was above, and what below.
Seminal powers made fertile mighty forces.
Below was strength, and over it was impulse.
But, after all, who knows, and who can say
Whence it all came, and how creation happened?
The gods themselves are later than creation,
so, who knows truly whence it has arisen?
Whence all creation had its origin,
the creator, whether he fashioned it or whether he did not,
the creator, who surveys it all from highest heaven,
he knows—or maybe even he does not know.

—Nasadiya Sukta, Rig Veda 10th mandala

3

"In the fourth part of Satya yuga, there ruled a king named Rathadhwaja with his wife Queen Padmini. Here is where we shall begin, O Maharani," Mahadev said to Draupadi.

"Before we begin with the good King Rathadhwaja and his queen Padmini, can you tell me the nature of reality, Mahadev? How did we all come to be? How was this world formed, O Great Lord?" the queen asked.

"I thought I knew what is real and what is not, but in the past while, my understanding of everything has been upended. I am not sure about anything anymore. You, O Lord, know the truth of all things: past, present, and those that are yet to pass. Would you, pray, share that knowledge with me, Shiv Shambhu?" Draupadi continued.

Mahadev grinned. It was only obvious the queen had questions.

"Maharani," he began, "the nature of reality is the nature of us all, the primordial spark that binds us all. It is *Brahman*, the Ultimate Reality of the universe, that has created and maintains us."

"What is *Brahman*, Mahadev?"

"*Brahman* is everything. It is within you and without. It exists everywhere, yet it cannot be seen, it can only be experienced. It is the eternal spirit, pure consciousness, indivisible, uncreated, and infinite. It does not change yet it is the cause of all things. It is the single binding truth which every being in this universe has emerged from and will one day dissolve into."

"How does the *Brahman* exist within us, Shiv Shambhu?"

"The *Brahman* manifests in yourself in the form of the *Atman* (soul). The *Atman* that is never changing, cannot be killed, nor can be destroyed. It is the seat of consciousness in every living being that propels them to a higher purpose. It is your *Atman*, Maharani, that has brought you here today, pushed you to seek answers, and resolve your soul's outstanding debts. With each lifetime, your *Atman* experiences what it needs to. Depending on your experiences and deeds, your next life can either be better or worse than the previous one.

The goal of the soul is to unite with its all-pervasive identity, the *Brahman*, the Ultimate Reality of the universe. When your *Atman* has dispelled ignorance, overcome desire, and realized the Supreme Truth, it stops seeking human form and your soul is released from the cycle of birth and death. You are then free from *samsara*, the circle of repeated birth and death due to karma and one with the Ultimate Reality."

"Will I ever be free from *samsara* and be able to unite with the Ultimate Reality, Mahadev?"

"Eventually, all humans will be able to unite with the Ultimate Reality. That is the conclusion of this universe. You too, Maharani, will be able to free yourself from this physical universe and unite with the Ultimate Truth. This journey that you are currently undertaking will help you achieve liberation, O queen."

"Tell me, Mahadev. How is *Brahman* different from the universe?"

"The *Brahman* is not different from the universe; it *is* the universe. It is the *Ekam Sat Vipra Bahudha Vadanti* which means 'Truth is one, although there are those who perceive it differently and call it by many names'. The *Brahman* is the One eternal principle, the unity behind everything, the ever-connecting bond, the light shining through us all, the Supreme Cosmic Spirit.

Once you realize the truth of the *Brahman*, you cease to identify yourself with your physical self and start relating to the *Brahman*. The wise say, '*Aham Brahmasmi*', or 'I am *Brahman'* because they know that nothing is apart from the *Brahman* for it resides in all of us. As Shri Krishna told your husband, Arjuna, when he was revealing the Bhagavad Gita to him, 'When the yogi develops the unified and holistic vision through the practice of yoga, he sees the Self in all and all in the Self'," Mahadev said.

"Explain to me the origin of creation, my Lord," the queen said.

Mahadev smiled. "In the beginning there was nothing except *Brahman*, that is ever existing and will never cease to exist. From this, came the *Hiranyagarbha* (the golden primordial egg), that floated on the endless ocean, upon which Vishnu rests. When it finally cracked, the cosmic power was released in the form of the Supreme Creator, Brahma, who then set about the task of creating this world.

There exist many worlds which are created by many Brahmas; all of which are floating upon the endless ocean. They exist unto themselves, with their own rules, their own physical laws, and their own form of life, not interacting with each other, until sometimes they collide releasing immense power enough to form a whole new world."

"How many such worlds exist, O Lord?" Draupadi asked.

"There are countless such worlds, all living their own form of reality, with the central truth of the *Brahman* within them. For even though they all exist separately, they will during the *mahapralaya*, the Great Dissolution, dissolve into the Supreme Reality so creation can begin anew," the Lord replied.

"On this world, Brahma's creation brought forth many mighty rulers—both queens and kings—who ruled for various periods of time. Some of them have been wise and just, others selfish and greedy. I believe you have experienced some of these greedy kings," Mahadev said.

Draupadi nodded. She knew very well the price of greed that King Dhritarashtra, the blind ruler of Hastinapur, had to pay. She too had paid a hefty price. The memory of her murdered sons made her sad.

"In the Shvetavaraha Kalpa," the Lord continued, "the third day of Brahma's year, after the beginning of the seventh Muhurtha, Maharaj Vaivashvata Manu was born. Following him, the great devotee of Lord Vishnu, King Ishvaku was born who ruled Satyawati; the land of Truth, for thirty-six thousand years.

This line of just rulers continued until the third phase of Satya yuga when Maharaj Sagar ruled for thirty thousand years."

"I see the years have diminished from King Ishvaku to Maharaj Sagar, although their times are greater than any ruler I have known of. Did that happen with every ruler after Ishvaku, my Lord?" Draupadi asked.

"Yes," Mahadev responded. "With each passing ruler, Satya yuga, the purest and truest of all yugas, started to lose its lustre until it ended after 1,728,000 years when Lord Vishnu took his avatar of Narsimha and killed the wicked King Hirayankashyapa. It is the holiest yuga not just because of the omnipresence of dharma but also because it was in Satya yuga that Lord Vishnu descended on earth four times; more than he has ever done since and will ever do again."

"What happened to the line of rulers after Maharaj Sagar, Mahadev?"

"Even though Maharaj Sagar had sixty thousand sons, his line continued with his grandson, Bhagirath."

"Why was that, O Lord? Were none of Maharaj Sagar's sons worthy?"

Mahadev smiled. "Perhaps they were not for they failed to recognize the great sage Kapila. See, Maharani, Maharaj Sagar was performing the Ashwamedha yagna when Lord Indra, afraid of the supremacy Maharaj Sagar would gain, stole all his horses, and left them at Sage Kapila's ashram who was deep in meditation. When the sixty thousand sons of Maharaj Sagar arrived at the ashram, they mistook Sage Kapila as the thief. Just as they were preparing to attack, the sage opened his eyes and burnt them all to ashes.

Consequently, the grandson, Maharaj Bhagirath became the ruler. This line continued unabated until King Vishvasaha came to the throne. During his time, adharma became rampant on Earth, greed started spreading and those in power began hoarding food, water, and all forms of wealth. Their voracity and looting were so atrocious that Earth fell under a famine that was three thousand years long.

With adharma all around, the kingdom of King Vishvasaha was completely destroyed, leaving only the just and wise behind. As time went by, the sages realized they needed rulers, so they gathered and visited Maharishi Vashistha who then conducted a maha yagna and manifested the next ruler, son of King Vishvasaha, King Khatvanga.

It is in this line of rulers, the ancestors of King Rathadhwaja, that we have come today. It is here that your story begins, Maharani," the Lord said.

King Rathadhwaja stood inside the newly finished temple marvelling at its grandeur. Located at the foot of dense green hills, the temple paid homage to the Supreme Goddess Durga, the deity of the primordial force and consort of Lord Shiva. King Rathadhwaja and his subjects were ardent followers of the Goddess. This newly erected shrine was yet another testament of their devotion for her.

Built entirely with gold, the temple was covered with intricate artwork and exquisite sculptures designed by expert artisans from all over the land. Every detail was created manually, including converting gold bars into foils, drawing the foils, and then mounting them on copper with each fragment methodically formed to share the knowledge and the significance of the Vedas.

With a unique construction of four shrines and towers, each shrine had a unique entrance through a porch with the roof supported by massive pillars covered with precious gemstones that glittered when the sun rays hit them and reflected the incandescent moon light. Pilgrims would walk a star shaped pathway to enter each of the shrines. Built in the middle of a lush green landscape, covered with exotic flowers, trees, and shrubs, the pathway was filled with spiritual messages, creation stories, and Vedic verses. The entire temple and adjacent courtyard had a presence of beaming energy designed to suck out the negative and infuse an effective, affirmative ambience.

King Rathadhwaja entered the main *garbhagriha* that formed the biggest shrine, in the centre of the temple where a lifelike idol of Goddess Durga stood amidst rays of sunlight pouring in. Seated on her tiger, the Goddess was adorned with a bright red sari, golden bangles, a diamond crusted nose ring, and several necklaces made with diamonds and other precious stones. Goddess Durga wore a large tiara made of gold with a fifteen-inch sapphire in the middle, bordered by eight inches of diamonds, emeralds, and rubies. Her many arms held her many weapons: a trident and a discus, as well as the lotus blossom and a conch shell. The Goddesses' shrine was adorned with flower garlands of the sweetest smell that spread their fragrance throughout the temple and its vast surroundings.

Gratified at her ferocious yet gentle image, the king bowed his head and paid homage to the Goddess, "O, Goddess Durga, I, your most ardent devotee, offer this temple and everything in it to you today. Please accept my sincerest offering and humble me, O Mother. In return I only ask, that you continue to shine your gracious presence and blessings on our kingdom," the king prayed.

King Rathadhwaja then returned to the courtyard and waited for the sages to begin the *mahasthapan* (official consecration ceremony), blessing the temple and opening it to the pilgrims. Throngs of visitors had already lined the temple walls to catch a glimpse of the king and offer their devotion to Ma Durga. Chants of *"Glory to Maharaj Rathadhwaja"* and *"Hail the Goddess Durga"* filled the air creating a spiritual atmosphere.

In all his splendour, the great sage Maharishi Atri sat in front of the sacrificial yagna, in the middle of the retinue of his sages, with King Rathadhwaja and Queen Padmini seated to his right. His long flowing hair tied into a bun, a lengthy white beard, a moustache, and a tilak on his forehead, the Maharishi glowed with the radiance of a hundred suns.

Setting intention, Maharishi Atri summoned Lord Agni and started with the *yagna diksha* or formal declaration to perform the ritual. With a silent nod, he then gave approval to the sages who began to chant hymns and songs from the *srauta* rituals inviting all the gods and goddesses to bless them. The introductory sages began their chants with "hum", followed by another group of who sang a fusion of melodies and Rig verses beginning with the sound "Aum". The last group of sages responded by singing the closing verse beginning with "hum".

And so, it continued for thirty days and thirty nights. The sages poured oblations, milk, vegetable cakes, stalks of plants and ghee, in the holy fire, uttering "Swaha!" invoking Lord Agni's wife to continue helping her husband to keep the fire going.

As the rays of the thirty-first morning hit the sacrificial party, Maharishi Atri, addressing the king and queen said, "Our rituals are now complete. We have blessed this temple and invoked all the Gods in the heavens for its protection. Now it is time for you to call upon the mighty Goddess herself."

The royal couple, accompanied by the great sage and his party, walked over to the second pit prepared for the generation of the *gārhapatya* fire. As Maharishi Atri and his entourage began the rituals once more, King Rathadhwaja and Queen Padmini started to pour oblations into the fire chanting the Goddesses' name.

As they continued their offerings, a divine voice spoke, "O great King Rathadhwaja and Queen Padmini, I am pleased with your devotion and piety. I bless you and your kingdom with prosperity and a long reign."

Realizing the voice belonged to none other than the Goddess herself, Queen Padmini replied, "O mighty Goddess, we are blessed with your presence here today. Would you be so kind to show us your physical form?"

Goddess Durga, a mirror image from her shrine in the temple, emerged from the lotus at the foot of the pit. The king and queen, along with Sage Atri, prostrated themselves before her.

"You have blessed me as well today, Mother," the great sage who possessed divine vision addressed the Goddess.

"Your life and your presence here are a blessing for all who are fortunate to be in your midst today, O Maharishi," the Goddess replied. "You have done the king and queen a great favour. I bless that your name shall be synonymous with good deeds and you shall receive the opportunity in this lifetime to serve the great Lord Vishnu when he takes human form in Treta yuga as Lord Rama."

The sage bowed, deeply grateful for the blessing.

Turning to the couple, the Goddess said, "This temple will be blessed for I shall reside in it. Your kingdom will prosper under your rule and you will experience the sweet taste of success. But, be careful, O king," the Goddess addressed Rathadhwaja, "to not let that sway your devotion and tempt you."

"Nothing shall ever tempt me enough to give up my faith in you, O Goddess," the king replied.

"If that is so, I will watch over you, your kingdom, and your reign. Every person who visits this temple will be under my protection. Because, I shall be in this temple for protection until it stands, I shall be known here as *Nitya,* the ever present."

The royal couple bowed and received the Goddess's blessing. Deeply content with the outcome, King Rathadhwaja and Queen Padmini returned to their palace, greatly honouring Maharishi Atri and all the other sages.

"King Rathadhwaja and Queen Padmini reigned the land of Satyawati for a long time. Their rule was successful and just. But, as time went by, the king started to change," Mahadev said to Maharani Draupadi.

"What sort of changes took place in the kingdom, my Lord?"

"Changes in the kingdom took place because of changes in the king. Let us take a look, shall we?"

King Rathadhwaja threw the plate of food to the ground. "How dare you tell me what to do?" he angrily responded to his prime minister.

"Maharaj," the nervous prime minister began. "The Choghadiya Muhurat on the fourth day of Kartika month, at sunrise is the best time for Durga puja. The royal astrologer has confirmed this time twice. He also said that a time like this only comes once every hundred years. It is the best time for us to conduct the puja ritual."

"I don't need anyone to tell me what time to do what," the king responded. "In fact, I don't even want to do a Durga puja ritual this year."

"But, Maharaj, how is it possible that you will not worship Goddess Nitya this year? You perform a big puja ritual every year in the Kartika month. Pray tell me, O great king, what has changed?" the prime minster asked, apprehensively.

"I don't need to tell anyone what has changed. But, since you ask, I will tell you. I am an extremely successful and wealthy king. The most powerful in this land, as a matter of fact. No king has yet forgotten the Ashvamedha yagna I performed five years ago. I am the indisputable ruler of this land. My harem is full, and I have two able bodied sons to carry my legacy forth.

I do not need to do a puja ritual to please a Goddess so she can continue shining her blessings on me. Truth be told, I do not need anyone."

The prime minister was aghast. How could his king, a fervent devotee of Goddess Durga, utter these words? Indeed, they were akin to blasphemy.

"My King, I shudder when I hear you speak these words. You are the most enthusiastic devotee of Goddess Nitya. How can you utter such words? Are you not afraid of the Goddesses' wrath?"

The king laughed heartily.

"Prime minister, you worry about things that do not matter. Goddess Nitya has many better things to do than worry about whether I worship her or not," he replied, dismissively.

"The Goddess would look after your kingdom and your reign until you were not swayed by temptation. Those were her words at the consecration ceremony. Surely, you remember them?" the prime minister reminded the king.

"Yes, I do. But, it is time to move on from all those things. It is time for me to take responsibility for our losses and credits for our gain. I am the irrefutable ruler of this land and it is because I am good at my job. Not because Goddess Nitya has blessed me."

"The king sounds arrogant, my Lord," Draupadi observed.

"The king *is* arrogant, Maharani," the Lord replied. "The king has forgotten that his good fortune and his mighty rule are the result of the blessings of Mother Durga. He has started to think he is responsible for his kingdom's prosperity. But, alas, this is the nature of humanity. Instead of vying towards their quest for *Atman*, the Supreme Reality, humans often fall prey for *ahamkara* or ego, the worldly manifestation of their position in physicality and possessions. Such a path, if not corrected quickly, can only lead to downfall."

"What really happens when humans get trapped in the ego, Mahadev?"

"When they get trapped, they get tied up in the cycle of birth and death. Only by killing the *ahamkara*, can the *atman* rise," the Lord explained. "The ego is what traps humans in suffering, enticing them to live in the temporary, ephemeral nature of this world. As a result, they forego the true nature of their soul and their self. *Ahamkara* is how the wise lose their way."

"Will King Rathadhwaja lose his way, Mahadev? What will happen to him?"

"The king's actions will determine his future, Maharani. It is only up to him."

Queen Padmini entered the royal chamber. King Rathadhwaja was already waiting for her.

"What is the meaning of keeping me waiting, Padmini?" the king demanded.

"I ask for forgiveness, O dear husband," the queen responded, "but I was busy with preparations."

"What are you busy preparing for?"

"What else can it be at this time other than our Kartika puja ritual for Goddess Nitya? We have chosen the freshest lotus flowers for the Goddess and the best devadasis from all over the land will be performing at the temple," the queen said with happiness in her voice.

"There is to be no puja this year, Padmini."

"What? No puja? Why? Is everything well, Lord?" the queen asked, shocked.

"Everything is well, and you heard me correctly. There will be no more pujas of any gods or goddesses in this land anymore. Not while I am the king."

"Pray tell me the reason, my dear husband."

"You do not need to know the reason. Know what your husband desires and make it happen," the king replied angrily and stormed out of the chamber, leaving a despondent queen behind.

"Forgive my husband, O Goddess for I do not know what has overcome him. We are still your devotees and we worship you with all our dedication. We know you are the *param shakti,* the eternal force, that drives this universe. I do not know what has happened to the king but please do not unleash your wrath on him, kind Goddess," the queen prayed her voice trembling with trepidation.

"Remember, I cautioned the king that such a day could arrive?" spoke a divine voice to Queen Padmini.

The queen knew who the voice belonged to. And, she did remember the warning that day of the temple consecration ceremony.

"I do, O Mother Durga. My husband has changed. His success and achievements mean more to him than his ardent worship of you. Pray tell me, what I can do to change his mind?"

"Let the king follow the path he has chosen, O queen. He predetermined his future even before he took human form. Let his soul learn what it needs to. Your soul, meanwhile, is pure but I am afraid walking this path with the king will lead to suffering for you too."

"I have chosen my path, O Goddess. My place is always next to my husband. I shall be his voice of reason and do my best to bring him back on this path of piety and *bhakti* (devotion)."

"*Tathaastu,*" the voice said, and the room turned still.

Queen Padmini sighed. She had a foreboding of what the future would bring.

King Rathadhwaja sat alone upon his royal throne in the dark court. His head in his hand, his eyes closed, the king for the first time felt afraid. All his might and bravado had been reduced to the constant worry lines on his forehead and the lack of sleep the king experienced from the repeated attacks of the Dasyus. In the past three years, the Dasyus had attacked seventeen times, each attack making the kingdom weaker. King Rathadhwaja was afraid his people could not survive this assault today.

His royal treasury almost depleted, the land was in chaos with severe food shortages everywhere. The king did not know where to turn. In his pride, he had discarded the advice of his family and well-wishers. When the Dasyus first attacked, the king in his over confidence, failed to mobilize the right plan and had to beat a hasty retreat. The poised Dasyus, out manoeuvred the king and his ministers, foiling their every plan, conquering more and more of King Rathadhwaja's land. In their most recent attack, the Dasyus had reached the temple of the mighty Goddess Nitya looting all the precious items, desecrating her shrines, and destroying the temple. King Rathadhwaja was losing his power. His kingdom was being destroyed by invaders.

The prime minister hurried with the royal family. They reached the court and found the king in deep thought.

"Maharaj, it is time to go," the prime minister said. "The enemy is at our doorstep. We must leave now so we live to fight another day."

The king raised his head and looked at the assembled party. His royal queen, who dressed in the best silk of the land, was now wearing garbs. His sons, the royal princes, looked like sons of commoners. The king could not believe his eyes. Tears flowed down his cheeks.

Walking up to the king, Queen Padmini wiped his tears, "Husband, let us go. It does not matter that we lose this kingdom today. What only matters is that we are alive, and we are together. You have two brave sons who will fight for your legacy and your kingdom. Let us not tarry any more. Come, my dear husband."

King Rathadhwaja looked away from the queen. He was embarrassed. The king knew he was the reason for their downfall. Clutching his queen's hands, he gently kissed them wetting them with his tears, "I should have taken your advice, my dear queen. I should have listened to you when you told me not to cast away Mother Durga. You have always stood by me and showed me the path of dharma, but I was blind. I was tempted by *Maya,* the illusion that exists around humans, Padmini. For that, I deserve the worst punishment. I shall bear the burden of my sins alone," the king said wailing.

"Take my sons and go to a place of safety. Our prime minister will keep you safe. Bring them up with devotion and love for the great Goddess Nitya for she is the only truth in this world. Everything else is fleeting."

"And what of you, my Lord?" the prime minister interjected.

"The king will remain here and guard his kingdom until he cannot," the queen spoke wiping her tears, her resolve firm. "He is a true warrior, and he will not abandon his throne. I make a vow to you, Nath, that I shall teach your sons the value of dedication and piety towards Goddess Nitya. Your death will not be in vain.

Your children will be good humans who will live virtuous lives and will serve their community."

The king blessed his sons as they departed the palace to a place of safety. King Rathadhwaja, then, sat on his throne, awaiting his ultimate end.

"Did the king die?" a curious Draupadi asked.

"The next morning, the invading army attacked the palace where they found the king. Wanting news on his sons, they tortured him, but the king did not divulge anything. Eventually, King Rathadhwaja died of his injuries," Mahadev said.

"That is a sad end to a mighty king," the queen said.

"One law this universe always abides by, Maharani, is everything we do, is met by an equally deserving outcome. In the case of King Rathadhwaja, his actions alone determined his consequences. He met a sorry end because he gave up the path of dharma and embraced his *ahamkara*. He died alone, without proper *samskara* (final rites), because of his love for his pride and his self. It is an unfortunate end, but one Queen Padmini knew and expected."

"What happened to Queen Padmini and her sons, Lord?"

"Queen Padmini and King Rathadhwaja had two sons: Dharmadwaja and Khushadwaja. The queen and the children hid in the forest and eventually joined Maharishi Atri's ashram, far away from their kingdom, who brought up the princes and looked after their education. Over time, the sons became proficient in scripts, languages, poetry, history, politics, literature, the puranas, and the Vedas.

Just as Queen Padmini had promised the king, the two sons grew up piously and became great seers. They were also ardent devotees of Goddess Nitya, who pleased with their worship, bestowed her blessings on them. The seers lived a comfortable life in the village with wont for nothing.

When they reached a marriageable age, their mother, the former queen, arranged suitable brides for both her sons. Dharmadwaja married Abhaya and Khushadwaja married Malavati. Their wedding was a time of celebration and festivities for the entire village who praised the former queen for her learned and accomplished children."

"Did the sons know of the circumstance of their father's death, Lord?"

"Yes, they knew," Mahadev said, his head nodding. "Queen Padmini wanted to make an example of her husband's life and how his pride led to his fall. She taught her sons the importance of devout devotion and the consequences when one abandons faith. Her sons learned from their father's death and performed intense penance and meditation to seek forgiveness from Mother Durga for their father's conduct.

They also conducted *pind daan* every year to help their departed father towards the path of salvation and lead him towards moksha," the Lord said.

"It sounds like the sons are doing everything right, Mahadev. So, why are we here then?" the queen asked.

"We are here because very shortly your story will begin in the home of Khushadwaja and Malavati. See,

Khushadwaja's intense penance and devoutness pleased Goddess Nitya. One day, as he was sitting down for his daily penance, Khushadwaja decided to invoke Lord Agni."

"Lord Agni? But, Khushadwaja's devoutness is towards Mother Durga. Why is he invoking Agni? Is he starting to lose his way like his father?" Draupadi asked puzzled.

"You Maharani are as impatient as Khushadwaja," Mahadev said, smilingly. "Your question is a valid one and will be answered in due time. Let us go see what happened next."

In the ashram courtyard, under a seat made of *kusha* grass, Khushadwaja sat in deep meditation. The first rays of the sun peeked through the horizon heralding a crisp and clear day, with a mild breeze blowing the leaves gently. Humming bees darted around; their mouths bursting with sweet nectar. The beaked chorus of birds filled the air. Several students already filled the ashram grounds working on their tasks for the day.

On the advice of Maharishi Atri, Khushadwaja started to pray to Lord Agni.

"It is time for you to invoke Lord Agni," Maharishi had told him.

His hands folded, Khushadwaja replied, "Maharishi, I will do as you command, however, Goddess Nitya is the source of my devotion. I am not sure I understand the reason for invoking Lord Agni."

"There are many things in this world that we are not sure of, Khushadwaja," the Maharishi said. "Let's just say the future of your family and of this world depends on your worship of Lord Agni and his grant of a boon."

Khushadwaja was intrigued. He decided to press the Maharishi further. "I would be honoured to serve in any way I can, Maharishi. What would Lord Agni have me do?"

"You have been a wonderful student and have become an accomplished rishi. I, however, see you are still struggling to learn patience and tolerance. Do not worry now about what Lord Agni would have you do, Khushadwaja. Instead, go invoke Agni and find out for yourself. Do not stop until Lord Agni has come to you."

A sheepish Khushadwaja bowed to his teacher and set out to follow the Maharishi's advice the next day.

"Om, let me meditate on the great flame, O God of fire, grant me with higher intellect, O let the radiant God of Fire illuminate my mind," Khushadwaja repeatedly chanted the Agni Gayatri Mantra.

Several hours passed. Khushadwaja's prayers continued. Day turned into dusk and dusk transformed into evening. Khushadwaja sat cross legged, his mind transfixed on Agni. In the third part of the evening, a bright orange light began to fill the courtyard where Khushadwaja sat. Gradually, the ruddy hued figure of Lord Agni started to emerge. With two faces, one beneficent and the other malignant, Lord Agni stood amidst the rishi with his three tongues, three legs, and seven arms. His glowing hair stood on end like flames, giving his entire appearance a cloudy, smoky tint.

"Open your eyes, O great rishi," Lord Agni spoke.

Khushadwaja opened his eyes and took in the splendid sight that stood before him. Bowing deeply, he paid the God his homage.

"O Lord of fire, friend and protector of humanity, I am blessed you chose to accept my prayers," Khushadwaja said.

"I always answer the prayers of those who call me with a pure heart. Your heart, O rishi, is pure and without malice. Ask for a boon, Khushadwaja," Agni said.

"Your sight is boon enough for me, O Lord. I wish no more from you," the awestruck Khushadwaja replied.

Lord Agni smiled. He knew why Khushadwaja had beckoned him. He also knew the rishi did not completely understand the purpose of his intense penance to Agni today. Regardless, Lord Agni knew what he had to do.

"You and your wife, Malavati, are good souls, rishi. Your path towards moksha is certain. However, in your human form you still have several responsibilities to complete."

"I am here to do whatever you command. Just say the word, O Agni Deva."

"I will but before I do so I have to ask you about Devi Sati. O Sage, tell me do you know of her?"

"I know of Dakshayani, O Agni Lord. But, what does she have to do with me?" a bemused Khushadwaja asked.

"If you know of her, you also know that when Daksha refused to give the great Lord Shiva his rightful place at the yagna, Devi Sati immolated herself."

"Yes, Deva, I know of Dakshayani's humiliation and her selfless sacrifice. I also know that it was Devi Sati who reincarnated as Mother Parvati, my most beloved and esteemed Goddess."

"So, here is what you do not know: when Devi Sati invoked me and entered the holy fire, a part of her stayed within me even after her rebirth as Mother Parvati. It is for this part of her that I have come here today."

"My entire existence will be privileged to help you with Devi Sati, my Lord. But, what would you have me do?" Khushadwaja asked.

"There is nothing for you to do, O Sage. I am here to do something for you," Agni said.

"Mother Parvati, who you call Goddess Nitya, is extremely pleased with your penance and your worship. She asked me to grant you a boon of her birth. The part of Devi Sati that stayed with me will be born in your home as your and Malavati's daughter. You and your wife, O Sage, will be parents to Mother Parvati's *ansh* (aspect) that she left behind with me during her immolation as Devi Sati. Glory be unto you, for you and Malavati are indeed the chosen ones!"

Khushadwaja was spellbound. This was an honour beyond his wildest dreams. He bowed to Lord Agni, profusely grateful for his boon and headed home to disclose the auspicious news to his wife, Malavati.

Khushadwaja looked at the little baby girl in the cradle. Although he knew who the little girl really was, Khushadwaja could not believe he and Malavati had created a being as beautiful as her. Touching her tiny feet with his coarse hands, the new father asked Mother Parvati for her blessing, thanking her for choosing him and Malavati as her parents.

"On this holy day, my life is fulfilled, O Mother. You have sanctified both, Malavati and I, with your ultimate blessing. Our lives are but to exalt in your holiness, however, today they have become even more singular in their devotion of you. We are honoured beyond words," Khushadwaja prayed to the little girl before him.

Cradling her gentle neck, Khushadwaja carefully lifted the baby and counted her fingers and toes—there were ten of each! Satisfied with his find, the protective father wrapped up his baby in linen and put her back down in the cradle for a nap.

On the twelfth day of her birth, Khushadwaja and Malavati held a naming ceremony for their little girl. True to protocol, the new parents assembled a variety of different objects to see where their baby girl would grant favour. Each time an object was placed in her cradle, the baby girl would turn away and start crying. Flowers, books, other items of religious significance were all placed next to her, but the little girl did not choose any of them. The confused parents did not know what else to do when Maharishi Atri entered their home.

Paying their respects to him, the couple told him of their dilemma. The Maharishi smiled.

"Of course, she refused everything. She would never have chosen any of those objects," he said.

"How shall we name her then, Maharishi? What would you advise?" Malavati asked, a puzzled look on her face.

"Bring me a copy of the Rig Ved," he told Malavati.

The great sage then took the oldest known Vedic text and placed it in the little girl's cradle. Immediately, the baby started to smile and kick up her legs in glee. Taking her right hand, she placed it on the Rig Veda as if eager to start reading.

The assembled party heaved a sigh of relief. Turning to them, the Maharishi said, "Vedavati. She will be known as Vedavati."

Draupadi exclaimed, "Ah, so here is how it all began. I am beginning to understand the significance of Lord Agni, Mahadev."

"Yes, as we go on more will become clear. But tell me, O queen, what are your impressions so far? What have you learned thus?"

Draupadi looked at Mahadev thoughtfully. "I am beginning to learn of the Supreme Truth, O Lord," she said after a few minutes of careful thought. "It is bigger than any human."

"And?" Mahadev prompted her.

"And, I am beginning to understand *ahamkara* and the corrosive role it can play in one's life."

"So, can you see how this relates to your current life?" Mahadev asked.

"Yes," the queen replied. "Yes, I most certainly can."

True to her name, Vedavati grew up with a penchant for the Vedas. By age five, she could recite the Sama and Atharva Vedas in their entirety. By age seven, she had conquered the Yajur and Rigveda as well. Khushadwaja and Malavati, though amazed at their daughter's feat, understood that her prowess was because she was none other than Goddess Durga herself. Every day Khushadwaja would look upon the innocent face of his daughter, exalting in the knowledge of her divinity.

Each morning, Vedavati would sit on a mat of *kusha* grass in the ashram courtyard, the same place her father was granted the boon of her birth by Lord Agni and continue her recitation of the Vedas. Humans, animals, birds, all of nature would stop their tasks to watch and hear Vedavati sing the most sacred hymns in her mellifluous voice. Eventually, people from all over the land started to hear about this precocious young girl with a prodigious gift. Kings from faraway lands travelled great distances to be in Vedavati's midst. Learned sages would be eager to catch a glimpse of this child they knew was holy. Even the Gods in *Swarga Loka* (heavens) could not help but admire Vedavati's talent and her utmost flair. Soon, every morning, the ashram would be flocked with men and women of all ages, even the Gods, yearning to hear Vedavati recite the Vedas and learn from her.

Vedavati's skills were matched only by her unparalleled beauty. The child grew up to be an exquisite woman, kind and empathetic towards all creatures. As she got older, her allure was noticed even more. With her long, shining, black hair, almond-shaped brown eyes, and an aquiline nose, Vedavati had a glossy complexion and a shapely body. Everyone, including Khushadwaja, could see how this young child was blossoming into a stunning woman. Khushadwaja knew he would have to find a suitable match for Vedavati soon, however, he was plagued with an impossible question: how does one choose a husband for the living incarnation of a Goddess? For every day, a new match would arrive at Khushadwaja and Malavati's doors; a new prince, a king, learned men, even many of the devas and the asuras were in love with Vedavati and wished to have her as their wife.

Khushadwaja and Malavati were in a quandary on whom to choose. While her parents debated their predicament, unbeknownst to them, Vedavati already had a husband in mind. But, she knew getting him to marry her would prove to be exceedingly difficult. Her mind, however, was made up and she knew what she would need to do.

One day, after her daily prayers in the ashram, Vedavati approached her parents.

"Dear father and mother, I have made a decision to visit Somnath," Vedavati informed them.

"Somnath? Why there during this time of year? The yearly fair is still a few months away, Vedavati. Won't you be too early for it?" her mother asked referring to the annual religious gathering held at the revered temple.

"I am not going for the fair, dear mother," Vedavati chuckled.

"If you are going for a *darshan* of the *Swayambhu,* perhaps I could accompany you," Malavati said, referring to the self-manifested Shiv Linga at Somnath that had made the temple so holy.

"No, dear mother. I must go alone. The time has come for me to marry. For that, I must choose a good husband. Somnath is where my search begins."

"Yes, indeed you must choose a husband," Khushadwaja replied. "We have been meaning to speak with you about the numerous proposals that have arrived."

"I know about them, dear father. But, I am afraid I must decline them all."

"All of them?" responded a surprised Khushadwaja.

"But, you don't even know all the proposals that are here. Some of them are devas from *Swarga Loka,* others are mighty kings. Still others are the most learned of all men in the land. How can you decline without knowing anything about them?" Malavati said.

"I know and I must. My fate is elsewhere," Vedavati said, firmly.

Khushadwaja sighed. He knew one day this day would arrive. But, he had hoped it would not be so soon.

"Where is your fate, dear child? Tell us and we shall do our best to help you," Khushadwaja said.

"But husband, she cannot just take off to Somnath leaving all these proposals behind," Malavati addressed her husband.

"Dear wife," Khushadwaja said, "don't forget the true essence of our child. She must do what she needs to, and we cannot stop her. Our only duty is to love and support her," he reminded Malavati.

Malavati looked resigned. She understood what her husband was telling her, but her motherly affection was refusing to let Vedavati go. Malavati realized though that she had no other choice.

Breathing deeply, she conceded. "I understand, dear husband. My love as a mother was blinding me to my real duty in this life. Tell us, Vedavati," she addressed her daughter. "What would you like to do?"

"My dear mother, I am the luckiest person in the world to have the unconditional love and affection of both my parents. How can I ever repay you for this understanding and thoughtfulness?" beamed Vedavati.

Malavati took her daughter's hands in her own. "You do not have to repay us for anything, my dear girl. Your birth is our salvation. We are lucky to have a daughter such as you and we will do everything we can to keep you happy. So, tell us, what can we do?"

"There is nothing for you to do, dear mother and father. What needs to be done, must be done by me alone. I shall leave for Somnath tomorrow morning and start my penance immediately."

Although he knew the answer, Khushadwaja asked anyway. "Who have you chosen as your husband, dear child?"

"The Lord of all Lords, Mahadev," Vedavati replied without a moment's hesitation.

Draupadi blushed, her frame stiffening up a little. Next to her, Mahadev felt her discomfort. He grinned. He could understand why the queen's body language had become slightly awkward.

"I can understand how you feel, Maharani, but there is nothing to be embarrassed about," he told her. Draupadi pursed her lips and smiled to herself. Of course, he thought that way.

Vedavati walked inside the temple at Somnath Prabhas. Even from where she was, Vedavati could hear the immense crash of the waves encumbered by the south seawall. She took in the power of the temple's beauty and its surroundings. Built entirely in gold by Lord Soma, the temple radiated under the shining sun. Nandi the bull; the gate guardian of Lord Shiva's abode Mount Kailash, stood at the temple entrance welcoming visitors. Vedavati walked from the central hall into the *antarala* (intermediate corridor) that led into the *pradakshina marga,* the circumambulatory passage around the innermost sanctum where devotees walk in a clockwise direction to receive the energies of the consecrated place in the best possible manner.

Four massive pillars lay connected by sculptural brackets in lintels: each standing at thirty-five feet from the other. The northern wall comprised of sculptures of elephants, men, horses carved in gold, whereas the southern wall greeted visitors with a massive carving of Mother Bhavani.

Throngs of pilgrims visited the temple everyday but today it was unassumingly quiet. After paying her respects to the *Swayambhu* Shiv Linga, Vedavati walked through the temple a few times taking in its vitality and warmth. From her earlier visits, she remembered the place to be a lot bigger but now that Vedavati stood amidst it, it looked substantially smaller. Or maybe it was she who had grown. Probably the latter, Vedavati thought smiling to herself. Old enough to choose a husband, she blushed.

Walking outside, Vedavati looked for a place where she could settle down for her penance. She soon found her spot underneath a banyan tree a mile away from the temple. Although amidst a forest, Vedavati chose the spot for its peacefulness and tranquillity. No one would disturb her here.

Sending a last prayer to her parents, Vedavati sat cross legged and closed her eyes to begin her intense meditation to please Lord Shiva so he would choose her as his bride.

"How did Vedavati's parents, Khushadwaja and Malavati, fare, O Lord? They must have found separation from their daughter difficult, isn't it?" Draupadi asked Mahadev.

"Khushadwaja and Malavati did not live for much longer after, O queen," he replied.

"Was separation from Vedavati too much to bear for them, Pashupatinath?" Draupadi asked, sadly.

"In a way, queen. You remember how Malavati had informed Vedavati about the various wedding proposals she had received?"

"I certainly do, Mahadev."

"Well, one of them was King Surya, who ruled a neighbouring land. When he found out that Vedavati had left for Somnath, King Surya flew in a fit of rage. In his anger, he arrived at the home of Vedavati's parents and killed them under a moonless night."

"Killed them?" gasped Draupadi. "Why such a heinous and excessive reaction, my Lord? Was King Surya not a kind ruler to resort to such violence that too to unarmed and such undeserving people?"

"King Surya was a good ruler but had an awfully bad temper. He also considered me a mendicant and did not allow anyone in his kingdom to worship me. So, when the woman he had fallen madly in love with rejected him for me, his anger knew no bounds."

"What an unfortunate end for the rishi and his wife," Draupadi lamented.

"Do not mourn Khushadwaja and Malavati's end, O queen, for their life was blessed with the birth of Goddess Durga as their daughter. After this life, Khushadwaja and Malavati were freed from the shackles of birth and death and found their salvation at the feet of their Goddess Nitya. Khushadwaja and Malavati, both realized their Ultimate Truth and became one with it."

Draupadi felt relief. Her parents from this birth had found their moksha.

"But, what happened to King Surya, Mahadev," she queried.

"King Surya eventually met an end befitting his crimes, Maharani. But, let us not spend any more of our time on him. Shall we return to Somnath?" Mahadev asked.

The queen acquiesced.

Vedavati's intense penance went on. Days turned to weeks. Weeks turned to months and months to years. Surviving with minimum food and water, Vedavati in due course gave up all forms of human needs, concentrating only on her pranas to reorganize her physiology and continue her task. The young woman sat under the banyan tree, uninterrupted by the world around her, doing everything she could to win Lord Shiva's heart. Wild beasts dared not harm her, humans left behind offerings but did not disturb her for fear of what her rage might do otherwise.

One day, several years after Vedavati had begun her penance, a brave warrior and mighty ruler visited

Somnath to offer his prayers to Lord Shiva. This fearless king, who commanded respect in all the worlds, a great Shiv devotee was taken by the temple and its beautiful atmosphere. He walked through Somnath experiencing a sense of calm and peace he had never before in his life.

"This temple is a special place," he told his minister after paying his respects to the *Swayambhu* Shiv Linga that manifested on its own. "We must visit Somnath often. I am so glad Sage Narada asked me to come here although I am not sure why he asked me to visit the forest."

"Strange are the ways of Sage Narada, O great king," the minister replied.

"Indeed. But now that I promised him, I would go to the forest, I must keep my word. Why don't you wait here for me, minister while I conclude my tour?"

"As you wish, Maharaj," the minister assented.

The king then walked from the temple to the adjoining forest thick with neem, peepal, and banyan trees.

"This king looks high and mighty, Mahadev. Who is he?" Draupadi asked.

"He is a great king, O queen. A kind, just, and wise ruler of his people. He is also a great scholar, a maestro of the veena and well-versed in mathematics, Vedas, urban design, and *Arthaśāstra*, the science of politics that he learned from none other than the great Sage Shukracharya.

This Maha-Brahman is not just a ruler of the most prosperous kingdom of his time, he is also a physician and has deep knowledge of ayurvedic remedies. Over time, he will write seven books on ayurvedic medicine that will be used throughout generations."

"He sounds remarkable," Draupadi said.

Mahadev nodded. "Yes, he indeed is. Do you see that flying craft over there?" Mahadev pointed to an object lying on the east side of the temple.

"I do, Mahadev," the queen replied straining her neck to see it.

"This king is the inventor of that object. It is called the Pushpak *vimana* (airplane) and the king you see before you is none other than King Ravana from Lanka," Mahadev said.

"Ravana?" Draupadi exclaimed. "That monster who kidnapped Sita and committed numerous atrocities? That Ravana?" Draupadi exclaimed, her hazel eyes wide with disbelief. "How can he be this remarkable ruler? He is an asura of the worst kind."

"He is not a monster, or an asura, nor did he commit any atrocities. He is a great ruler, one of my biggest devotees who simply fell for the wrong woman. But, that too is not on him. He only played a pre-ordained part in the grand scheme of this universe," Mahadev explained, calmly.

"My trust in you, Mahadev, surpasses everything but this is Ravana we are talking about," Draupadi replied, reluctantly.

"You will see, Maharani. You will soon see Ravana's true nature and his doomed fate that he himself agreed to."

"You mean Ravana knew what would happen to him?" the queen asked, incredulously.

"Not only did he know, but he also picked his end, himself," Mahadev replied. "But, that story is for another time. Let us return to Vedavati for now."

Ravana walked through the lush green forest enjoying its beauty. Tall trees touched the sky with sun rays penetrating through, dancing on the forest floor. Bees happily hummed about from one blossom to the next, while the sambar deer ambled around with their long, slender legs and compact torsos. Ravana could smell the wildflowers mixed with an earthy smell of the forest as he made his way deeper inside, branches creaking under his strong feet.

Soon, Ravana came upon the banyan tree where Vedavati was seated. Wearing the hide of a black antelope, Vedavati's dark, shining, black hair had matted in a *jata* (dreadlock) like a seer. Already inexpressibly beautiful, Ravana could see Vedavati's youth shining through, enhanced by her penance. He was immediately taken by her beauty, her devotion, and her intensity.

Getting down on his knees, Ravana invoked his deep energies and bowed to Vedavati, "O, great lady, please open your eyes."

Vedavati's penance was interrupted. She opened her eyes, expecting to see the sight of Lord Shiva. Instead, she saw a formidable man with several wound marks all over his arms and chest. He appeared in robust health, with a strong physique and all his organs proportionally framed. He wore a golden silk dress matched with a heavy crown and dazzling jewellery.

"What is the meaning of this interruption?" Vedavati demanded.

"O great lady, my name is Ravana, and I am the king of Lanka," he replied.

"I did not ask who you are or where you are from," Vedavati responded angrily. "I asked, 'What is meaning of this interruption?' Why have you disturbed me?"

"I apologize for disturbing you, O great one, but I was here to visit the temple of Somnath and pay respects to the great Lord Shiva. After, I decided to enter the forest and came upon you. Taken by your magnificence and intensity, I decided to wake you. My intention was not to disturb you in any way."

"Yet, you *did* disturb me but considering that you are a Shiv devotee I am willing to let you speak. Now tell me why you disturbed me."

"You are the fairest and the most beautiful of all women I have ever seen in this world. Your beauty, your devotion, and your passion are strong enough to sway even the mightiest of Gods. I am only a human and I too am swayed by you. Come with me, O great lady. Marry me and make me the luckiest man ever to live. I will provide you with all the riches of this world, both known and unknown."

Vedavati softened. "Your words humble me, O Ravana, but I cannot marry you for I have already chosen a husband in my heart."

"Your words are breaking my heart, O lady. But, since you have already committed yourself to someone, I shall not press this matter any further. Humble me with the knowledge though. Tell me the name of the lucky person who shall receive your love and devotion."

"It is the Lord who resides in both our hearts, O King. Lord Mahadev is in my chosen one and I shall only marry him."

"I do not but stand a chance with Lord Mahadev. O great lady, you have made the perfect choice for there is no other stronger or better than him in all the worlds. I wish you all the happiness with the great Lord," Ravana said, sadly.

Ravana got up to leave. Vedavati stopped him. "O great king, it gives me great sadness to tell you this but before I sat down to conduct my penance, I took a vow to curse anyone else besides Mahadev should they disturb me. My penance is broken, and the purity of my intentions has been destroyed. You are a wise king, but you were swayed by my ethereal beauty not my spiritual goal. In accordance with the vow I took, I must now curse you, O great king."

Ravana looked despondent. He was beginning to understand why Sage Narada had requested he visit the temple and the forest.

Ravana smiled. "We are all but players in a game controlled by the Supreme God. I believe my fate was pre-ordained, O great lady, and I was destined to be here today. I shall not stop you from doing what you need to and face my destiny with my full responsibility," the wise king replied. "But, before you proceed to curse me, may I make one final request of you, Devi?"

Vedavati nodded.

"Please do not waste your powerful spiritual energy by cursing me. Instead, become the cause of my death in your next lifetime. I shall feel redeemed by your presence in my life once again and consider myself among the luckiest of men to die because of you," the king beseeched.

Vedavati pondered on Ravana's suggestion. She understood why he was asking her to do that.

Vedavati assented to Ravana's request. "Very well, O King. I shall be the cause of your death in my next birth. But, since I am taking the easy way out, I shall no longer continue with my penance and walk into the fire."

"O Devi, please do not become a sati on my accord. I shall not be able to live with that obligation," Ravana implored to Vedavati.

"I assented to your condition, O Ravana. If I am not going to use my *siddhi* (paranormal power) to curse you, I must stop gathering any further energy and disseminate everything I have into the fire. That is its rightful place. Since I have already agreed to be the cause of your death, I must now follow through on my word and enter the holy fire."

Although it made him inexplicably sad, Ravana conceded. He knew he would not be able to change the lady's mind.

"It is a fateful day when I walked here today. We both know now how we meet our end. Before I leave, would you be kind enough to tell me your name, O divine woman?" Ravana asked.

Vedavati smiled gently. "My name is Vedavati."

"Vedavati, I thank you for this experience today. I shall never forget you and shall wait for you to receive my end. Although your presence in my life once more will mean my death, I can hardly wait to see you again."

With that, the king bowed to Vedavati and returned to his Pushpak *vimana*. With an image of Vedavati in his heart, Ravana returned to Lanka waiting for the moment he would see her again.

Alone in the forest again, Vedavati started to invoke Lord Agni.

"O Vedavati, why have you summoned me? What can I do for you?" Lord Agni asked.

Vedavati grinned. "This is beginning to look familiar, Agni Deva," she told him referring to her summon of him in lives past from ancient times.

"Does your human form remember who you previously were?" Agni asked.

Vedavati smiled. It had been a long and happy life but in these final moments she started to remember who she truly was.

"I could not achieve the purpose my heart desired, Agni Deva," she said.

"You could not, but you achieved an even greater purpose, O Mother. Your love and devotion of Lord Shiva is unmatched in all known and unknown universes. There is no greater bond than the bond between the two of you. Yet, there are things that both you and Lord Shiva must do. Your sacrifice is immense, but you are the force behind everything and so when the world needs you, you do what you must," Agni explained.

"Ravana is a good king. I dislike that I will be the cause of his death."

"You are only doing what is pre-ordained. Now command me, Mother. What can I do for you?"

"You know what you must do. I came from you and now I must return unto you."

"I am privileged and honoured, Mother. But, is there no other way for you to continue your penance in this lifetime?"

"No, there is not. I am afraid this is the end, however, before I leave there is something I must do."

Using her yogic powers, Vedavati shed her hair on to the ground. Lord Agni looked at her puzzled.

"My hair has accumulated enough power to protect this earth from evil and misdeed until I return again," Vedavati explained. "Now, it is time."

Vedavati entered the fire and disappeared amidst the flames.

Mahadev sighed. Even though he had seen it countless times, it was never easy to watch Vedavati self-immolate.

Draupadi was in tears. She could not believe her own eyes. Pure acceptance by Ravana no matter the consequences for him. Pure courage by Vedavati in not taking the easy way out. Draupadi's heart was so full it could burst any minute.

She could feel Vedavati's pain for it was her own. She could feel the sheer willpower with which Vedavati acted for she had as well. She knew her grief, her deep anguish. She was beginning to see more than just her. Draupadi was meeting her trauma head on, unflinching. Drenched in her own tears, the queen for the first time in her life felt lighter than she had since Krishna's death.

Wiping her wet face with her sari, Draupadi composed herself and turned to face Mahadev who was patiently waiting for her, his eyes shining with kindness and compassion.

"I have one question, Mahadev," the queen said, her eyes brimming with tears again.

"Ask, Yajnaseni," Mahadev replied.

"Why did Vedavati not curse Ravana? Why did she choose to instead be the cause of his death instead?"

Mahadev smiled. "Ravana was a Maha-Brahman, a learned man just like Vedavati. He knew the strength and power of Vedavati's penance. He understood the force of good her energy could be for the world. If Vedavati were to curse someone as educated and pious as him, she would have used a substantial portion of her power in doing so. Ravana saw that as a waste and instead suggested she become the cause of her death.

This way, although Vedavati would disseminate her energy into the fire, she could call upon it whenever she needed it. It was also why she was able to leave her hair behind for the world's protection. None of that would have happened had Ravana not suggested thus."

Draupadi nodded.

"There is one other thing that Ravana's suggestion helped you do," Mahadev said.

"Me? You mean me as Vedavati, Mahadev?"

"No, Maharani. I mean you as Draupadi, wife of the Pandavas," Mahadev stressed.

"What could Ravana's suggestion possibly have to do with me as Draupadi, Mahadev?" the queen asked bewildered.

Mahadev took a deep breath. He pondered if it was the right time to divulge this knowledge. Mahadev knew at some point he would have to let Draupadi know of her deep connection with Ravana. But, now was not that time. Perhaps he was not the right person to reveal it either, Mahadev thought.

"We will talk about it at some other point," he replied to the queen.

Draupadi's curiosity was piqued but she decided not to press the matter.

"So, what happened to Ravana after Vedavati died, Mahadev?" Draupadi asked changing the subject.

"Ravana returned to Lanka and mourned Vedavati for months. When he finally emerged from his chamber, he decided to visit Somnath again. Ravana's experience at Somnath had so transformed him that that he spent a considerable fortune making additions to the temple, all in pure silver. He erected four more pillars inside the temple and built the temple's east and west walls. On the western wall he had artisans carve the unforgettable image of the divine woman engraved upon his heart," Mahadev, who knew of heart break very well, said with sadness in his voice.

"I misunderstood Ravana, Mahadev. He is more than I ever imagined to be."

"He indeed is, Maharani."

"Why is he so misinterpreted then, Shiv Shambhu?"

"People like to see the world as black and white, Draupadi. They do not understand grey although all humans operate in the middle. The day humans understand, they will stop using labels such as 'good', 'bad', 'evil'. You are grey, your husbands are grey, Lord Shri Krishna was grey, Karna, Duryodhana, everyone who wronged you was both good and bad.

Good people do bad things because that is the nature of humanity. In our desire to seek villains and hold someone solely responsible for events, we only start to advance their bad deeds and eventually we misinterpret them from who they truly are."

"Was the Kurukshetra war a result of people being both good and bad?"

"The Kurukshetra war was a result of accumulation of adharma. It was time to cleanse the world of the collective evil that was taking place. It was a war in which both good and bad people died. People like Bhishma, Dronacharya, Karna were learned men who knew they were operating on the wrong side. But, in the end, they were good people."

Draupadi was beginning to understand.

"I am pleased to see our journey so far is helping, Yajnaseni. What we see next should alleviate many more doubts and questions for you."

"Where are we going next, Mahadev?"

"To Ayodhya to witness the birth of Lord Vishnu's avatar, Shri Rama," Mahadev replied.

Part III

Chaya

(Hanuman said:)

1.1: O Devi Janaki, I salute You; You are the destroyer of all Sins,

2.1: (I Salute You) You are the destroyer of Poverty (in the battle of life) and bestower of wishes of the Devotees,

2.2: (I Salute You) You are the daughter of Videha Raja (King Janaka), and cause of Joy of Raghava (Shri Rama),

3.1: I Salute You, You are the daughter of the Earth and the embodiment of Knowledge; You are the Auspicious Prakriti,

3.2: (I Salute You) You are the destroyer of the Power and Supremacy of (oppressors like) Ravana, (and at the same time) fulfiller of the wishes of the Devotees; You are an embodiment of Sarasvati,

4.1: I Salute You, You are the best among Pativratas (Ideal Wife devoted to Husband), (and at the same time) the Soul of Janaka (Ideal Daughter devoted to Father),

4.2: (I Salute You) You are very Gracious (being Yourself the embodiment of) Riddhi (Lakshmi), (Pure and) Sinless, and extremely Beloved of Hari,

5.1: I Salute You, You are the embodiment of Atma Vidya, mentioned in the Three Vedas (Manifesting its Inner Beauty in Life); You are of the nature of Devi Uma,

5.2: (I Salute You) You are the Auspicious Lakshmi, the daughter of the Milky Ocean, and always intent on bestowing Grace (to the Devotees),

6.1: I Salute You, You are like the sister of Chandra (in Beauty), You are Sita Who is Beautiful in Her entirety,

6.2: (I Salute You) You are an Abode of Dharma, full of Compassion and the Mother of Vedas,

7.1: (I Salute You) (You as Devi Lakshmi) Abide in Lotus, hold Lotus in Your Hands, and always reside in the Heart of Shri Vishnu,

7.2: I Salute You, You reside in Chandra Mandala, You are Sita Whose Face resembles the Moon

8.1: (I Salute You) Your Form gives Joy to all, You are the Sati (Devoted Wife) whose presence is Auspicious and confers Siddhi and Liberation,

8.2: I Salute the Mother of the Universe, Who is the Beloved of Ramachandra,

8.3: I always Worship You in my Heart, O Mother Sita, You are Beautiful in entirety, the Beauty which cannot be expressed in words.

—*Janaki Stuti*, by Tulsidas

4

"Mahadev, could you tell me more about Ravana? I still cannot believe who he really was and how time has misunderstood him," Draupadi addressed the Lord.

"Humans have misunderstood him, Maharani, not time. Time does not indulge in any actions. It is a silent spectator, recording everything but divulging nothing. It is infinite, cyclical, and it will never stop until the Great Dissolution when everything will be absorbed in the Absolute.

Since you ask, though, I will tell you more about Ravana. He is one of the most misunderstood rulers of any time but just like any other human, he had both good and bad in him.

But, before I tell you about Ravana, let us talk about his land, Lanka, for one cannot be understood without understanding the other.

Shortly after he created all beings, a satisfied Brahma decided to take a nap. The newly formed world was excited and buzzing with energy. Many of the new creatures wanted to visit Brahma and thank him for taking on this arduous task.

Among them were two amphibians, Heti and Preti. They walked up to Brahma's home but were stopped by his guards. Heti and Preti got very loud, which woke Brahma up. Furious, he went out to see the source of the commotion and found Heti and Preti beating up his guards. In a fit of rage, Brahma cursed them to live on Earth and suffer as humans do.

Heti and Preti started living on Earth but since they were amphibians, they needed a place where there was both land and water side by side. They searched for a while but could not find something that they both liked. That is when Heti and Preti decided to pull a piece of land from underneath the sea. This land, surrounded by water on three sides, became their home and came to be known as Lanka.

Heti and Preti had a sister, Kaikesi, who visited them often. Once when Kaikesi was visiting them in Lanka, the great sage Vishrava, son of Pulastya and grandson of Brahma was meditating on their lands. Kaikesi, angry with Brahma for cursing her brothers, seduced the great sage and a son was born from their union, Dasamukha.

Over time the couple produced three other children: two sons, Kumbhakarna and Vibhishana, and a daughter Minakshi, later called Surpankha. But, it is their eldest son, Dasamukha who stood apart from every other human in the world. Not only was he an unparalleled scholar but his physical prowess was also unmatched."

"But, I thought Kumbhakarna and Vibhishana's brother's name was Ravana," Draupadi asked. "So, then who is Dasamukha?"

Mahadev nodded. "Dasamukha *is* Ravana. It was his real name before I coined the name Ravana for him."

"*You* named him Ravana, Mahadev?" Draupadi asked, genuinely puzzled.

Mahadev laughed. "Yes, I did."

Draupadi smiled. "Why?"

"I named him Ravana after he let out a huge shuddering cry of pain. See, Maharani, one day I was hunting when Ravana passed through the mountains of Saravana. Nandi, my guard, would not let Ravana pass so he became incredibly angry and started to shake the mountain with his mighty arms.

I had to place a single toe to stop the shaking and steady the mountain which fell on Ravana's arms. That is when he let out a cry that gave him his name. After one thousand years of worship, I released Ravana from his predicament of carrying the mountain and named him thus. It was after this that he also became my biggest *bhakt* (devotee)."

"Ah, that is such an enchanting story. No wonder Ravana never goes against you," Draupadi said laughing.

"No," Shiva joined her. "No, he won't. But, that is not why. The real reason lies in the purity of his soul and the genuineness of his intentions."

"You are very fond of Ravana, are you not, Mahadev?"

"I am fond of anyone who worships me with a pure heart, Maharani. Ravana is just one of them."

"So, tell me the story behind Ravana's heads, Mahadev. The prevailing norm is his ten heads were the result of his evil nature, but something tells me there is another purpose behind them," the queen said, perceptively.

Ravana was not evil, he was enormously gifted. He was a great Vedic scholar with immense intellectual capabilities. Ravana's ten heads symbolize the four Vedas—Rig-Veda, Sama-Veda, Yajur-Veda, and Atharva-Veda and the six Shastras—Sankhyashastra, Yog, Nyayashastra, Vaisheshik, Purvamimansa, and Uttar Mimansa. His ten heads do not mean the negative aspects of the human mind but the good that he accumulated in his lifetime in terms of learning and education. There was not nor there will be a bigger Maha-Brahman than Ravana.

He was such an absolute ruler that when Kubera, the king of Lanka, saw him he was convinced there could be no greater king on Earth. Kubera willingly gave up his kingdom to Ravana so Ravana could be the just and mighty ruler Kubera knew he would."

"And, Ravana did not disappoint," Draupadi said.

"No, he did not," Mahadev replied shaking his head. "Lanka flourished and prospered during Ravana's rule. Ravana was a just ruler but he was also extremely shrewd. He was a strategic military leader and proceeded on a series of campaigns conquering humans, celestials, and demons. You already saw his Pushpak *vimana* that Ravana designed himself."

Draupadi nodded.

"He also possessed a trained navy. Ravana was an expert warrior and introduced several new techniques among his soldiers like wearing camouflaged headgear in battlefield; procedures that are adopted routinely in war now.

Ravana was a benevolent leader who ruled a highly advanced civilization. He was an expert architect and built magnificent homes using costly timber for his subjects. This was partly why Hanuman could so easily set them on fire.

Ravana's palace was a staggering piece of architecture. His central palace-complex was a massive collection of several networks of palaces that reached over one yojana (13 km) in height, one yojana in length, and half a yojana in breadth. Glittering with precious gemstones and other riches, Ravana's palace was like heaven upon earth, effulgent with glory, embedded with diamonds, covered by flowers of various trees.

King Ravana was an expert among warriors; a specialist among medical men; a seer among astrologers; a superior statesman among rulers; and a maestro among musicians. There was nothing he could not do."

"How long did he rule, Mahadev?"

"Ravana ruled for two thousand years and would have continued for thousands more had he not made the biggest mistake of his life."

"Kidnapping Sita."

"Yes, his pre-ordained kidnapping of Sita."

"You said earlier that Ravana knew of this end, that he even chose it. How is that Mahadev?"

Mahadev paused thoughtfully. "The story of Ravana's avatars is the story of Lord Vishnu's gatekeeper."

"Lord Vishnu's gatekeeper? What does one have to do with other? Ravana was a powerful king but what could he have to do with Lord Vishnu?"

"I see, Maharani, that you have not yet been able to reconcile your previous impression of Ravana with your newfound knowledge about him. You still think him less than."

Draupadi looked away from Mahadev embarrassed with the battle raging in her heart. For it *was* true, she was still struggling because accepting Ravana as a good ruler, a wise king, and a great scholar would mean she would have to accept the idea of good people doing bad things. This would not be so hard to reconcile if it would not mean extending that same courtesy to Duryodhana, Dushashan, and Karna, her arch enemies.

A courtesy that, in Draupadi's mind, was impossible to extend and completely undeserved. For she could still remember that day and the vivid pain, and degradation she felt over the senseless act of her disrobing amidst the entire court full of Earth's mightiest heroes and learned men. She could not forget how she, a woman, was used as a pawn to satisfy the unyielding desire of men and how no one came to her aid! How no one acted to stop her humiliation, cover her bare body, and take her away. No one except her Gopī-jana-vallabha! Draupadi could have cursed them all, every single person in that court, including her husbands, had it not been for the timely intervention of Duryodhana's mother, Gandhari. No, she was not ready to extend any forgiveness to the Kauravas or to Karna.

The fire within her started to burn ferociously yet again.

Mahadev saw Draupadi's dilemma. He understood her pain but chose to not address it. Not yet at least. Draupadi needed more time and more information. He hoped once she saw it all, Draupadi would come to the realization herself. He knew that nothing more he could say or do would relieve the queen of her grievances.

So, instead he proceeded with his tale.

"A long time ago, four Kumaras who were thousands of years old, arrived at the palace of Lord Vishnu. Because of the intensity of their penance though, they looked like young children. Thinking the kids were up to no good, Vishnu's gatekeepers Jaya and Vijaya did not allow them entry to see the Lord. This angered the Kumaras who cursed the gatekeepers to be born on Earth and suffer human trials and tribulations.

The gatekeepers were very distressed and asked Vishnu to lift the curse but the curse of the Kumaras once cast, can never be lifted by anyone, no matter how powerful. The guards had no choice but to be born on Earth. Vishnu, however, could give them two options: be born on Earth seven times as devotees of Lord Vishnu or be born on Earth three times as his enemy and be killed by him who would take human form to destroy them. The choice was easy for the two guards—they did not want to bear the pain of being parted from the Lord for seven lifetimes, so Jaya and Vijaya chose to be born as Vishnu's enemies three times."

"Oh, that is truly incredible. So, who were they born as and when?" Draupadi asked.

"They were born in Satya, Treta, and Dwapara yugas. In Satya yuga, they were born as Hiranyakashipu and Hiranyaksha, killed by *Varaha,* Vishnu's boar avatar and *Narasimha,* the man-lion avatar. In Treta yuga, they were born as Ravana and Kumbhakarna, and were killed by Rama. In their third and final life during Dwapara Yuga, they were born as Dantavakra and Shishupala and were killed by Krishna. After their three lifetimes, they were reunited with Lord Vishnu and stand today guarding his gates once again.

I believe you witnessed the death of Shishupala, did you not?" Mahadev asked.

"I did, Mahadev. It occurred at Yudhisthir's Rajasuya yagna when Shishupala insulted Lord Krishna and the Lord killed him with his Sudarshan Chakra."

"It was also when Lord Krishna promised to always come to your aid, did he not?"

"Yes," Draupadi smiled. "After I tore off a piece of my sari to bandage his wounded finger, Lord Krishna promised he will always be there for me. And, he always was. He was my only friend and confidant." The memory of her deceased friend brought tears to Draupadi's eyes. "This world is too much to bear without him, Mahadev. Nothing is worth it without Krishna's friendship and his presence." Draupadi sobbed softly, the pain wrenching her heart.

"I can understand how you feel, Maharani, but life must continue no matter who leaves us. That is the nature of living. Earth has seen so many great lives pass but she does not stop moving because that is her work. Similarly, humans need to keep living, keep working for that alone is our salvation," Mahadev explained.

"What do we work for though, Mahadev, if those we love are taken away from us?" the queen asked.

"We work for ourselves, Maharani. We work *on* ourselves for true work is the only redeemable path. Lord Krishna himself recommended the course of karma yoga. For that person who engages in selfless action, focusing only on the intention without worrying about the result, achieves salvation.

The meaning of Karma is in the intention. The intention behind the action is what matters. Those who are motivated only by desire for the fruits of action are miserable, for they are constantly anxious about the results of what they do.

The Lord said: "*Karmanye Vadhikaraste Ma Phaleshu Kadachana, Ma Karma Phala Hetur Bhur Ma Te Sango Stv Akarmani*" which means "You have every right to work but no right to expect the fruits out of it. Let the focus not be on the fruits but the selfless action and never be inactive."

And, never forget, regardless of who and what you are, always work. That is the best path forward for all beings in this universe."

Ayodhya was ripe with anticipation for the yagna. The only topic of discussion in the entire city seemed to be who would take over the throne next. Although King Dasharatha was young and would rule for many more years, he had no heir. None of his three queens Kausalya, Kaikeyi or Sumitra could produce the child the kingdom desperately sought.

The king and his queens had tried everything—physicians from faraway lands made the queens and the king drink their concoctions, sages were invited to bless them, fertility gods were invoked but nothing worked. The king and his three queens continued to remain childless.

Desperate to have an heir, King Dasharatha finally decided to seek the counsel of Saptarishi Vasishtha, the priest and teacher of the Ikshvaku clan. Early one morning, after performing his daily ablutions, the king along with his three queens entered the most revered Vedic rishi's ashram.

"O Great Sage, I, Dasharatha, seek your advice and help."

"King Dasharatha, to what do I owe this honour?" a curious Sage Vasishtha responded.

"You know of all our travails, O Saptarishi. It has been many years since my wedding to my three queens but alas, my kingdom remains without an heir. Pray tell me, O Sage, how must I produce an heir who may carry forth my legacy?"

"You come to a sage to ask for marital advice, O King?" the Sage teased him.

"O Rishi, I come to you because you have the answer to all the queries in this universe. Please, tell me what I must do to continue the Ikshvaku clan."

The Saptarishi smiled. Yes, he knew the answer to the king's query.

"O great king, it is time for you to perform the Putrakameshti yagna. For this, you will need a sage who is expert in Yajurveda which has the guidelines for this ritual."

"Where do I find this sage, O Saptarishi?" the king inquired with hope in his heart.

"There is no one in this world who knows the Yajurveda better than Maharishi Atri. Go seek him at the Girnar Ashram near Somnath temple. He will aid you," Sage Vasishtha replied.

The king and his queens bowed to the Saptarishi and returned to their palace. The next day, King Dasharatha set off for Somnath.

King Dasharatha was awed by the sight of Somnath. Built in gold and silver, the temple was crowned by a fifteen metre-high *shikhara* that hoisted its flag on the top. Its four massive walls were engraved with mesmerizing artwork and sculptures of various devas and apsaras. After paying homage to the *Swayambhu,* self-manifested Shiv Linga, King Dasharatha walked around the temple awed by its stupendous presence, stunning glory, and breath-taking views of the roaring waves.

Considering himself fortunate for being able to visit Somnath at its prime, Dasharatha eventually reached the ashram of Maharishi Atri. Prostrating himself at the rishi's feet, the King informed the sage the purpose of his visit.

"I have been sent to you by the great Saptarishi Vasishtha, O Sage," the king said. "Sage Vasishtha has asked me to perform the Putrakameshti yagna so I may carry forth my legacy and my dynasty. Please help me, O Maharishi Atri," the king pleaded.

"Get up, O mighty King Dasharatha. I have been waiting for your arrival for a long time for it means the beginning of many fortunate events. It would be my honour to help you perform the Putrakameshti yagna. Let us choose an auspicious date for this most blessed occasion. I am sure after this yagna is performed, Lord Agni will be pleased with you and grant you the favour you so desperately seek," Maharishi Atri replied.

And so, it was determined that the yagna would take place on the sixth day of the Shukla Paksha during the month of Chaitra. A special *mandap* was built on the palace grounds to enable the royal party along with Maharishi Atri and his retinue to perform the ritual.

When the auspicious day finally arrived, King Dasharatha, the son of King Aja of Ayodhya and Apsara Indumati of *Swarga Loka*, sat next to his three wives and Maharishi Atri, ready to perform the *kaamya* karma, and invoke the blessings of the Supreme Creator of the world, Lord Vishnu, through the intervention of the fire.

Reciting the Purusha Suktam, Maharishi Atri began by singing the sixteen verses glorifying Lord Vishnu as the ultimate Purusha and a celestial being with infinite heads and feet, describing how different species came into being from his body parts. The Maharishi's recitation was accompanied by sages pouring milk, fruits, sweets, holy water, coconut, and ghee into the fire.

"ōṃ tacchaṃ yōrāvṛṃīmahē / gātuṃ yajñāyá / gātuṃ yajñapátayē / daivī svastirástu naḥ / svastirmānuṣēbhyaḥ / ūrdhvaṃ jigātu bhēṣajaṃ / śaṃ nō astu dvipadē / śaṃ chatuṣpadē / ōṃ śāntiḥ śāntiḥ II," the Maharishi repeated the verse in its entirety repeatedly. As he continued his singing, the fire began to glow brighter with a dark hue. Soon, the crimson figure of Lord Agni started to appear.

Bowing to him, the royal party and the sages offered Lord Agni their respects.

"Lord Vishnu is pleased with you, King Dasharatha," Lord Agni said addressing the ruler of Ayodhya. "He knows what you desire and will be pleased to fulfil your wish."

King Dasharatha smiled, relieved at hearing the Lord's words.

"I am most grateful to both you and Lord Vishnu, O Agni Deva," the king said, his hands folded in prayer position. "I, the Lord's most humble servant, will forever remain in his eternal debt."

"You do not owe the Lord any debt, O King. The Lord has chosen you for a reason. This is the Lord's *Leela*, his divine play," Lord Agni said.

The god of fire then handed a bowl of sweet porridge to each of Dasharatha's wives. Addressing them he said, "Eat this in its entirety and you will be blessed with a child." Kausalya, Kaikeyi, and Sumitra accepted the bowl, bowing to the Lord for his generosity.

The royal party was content. Their prayers were finally answered.

On the ninth day of Chaitra, when the presiding deity of ruling star was Aditi and four of the nine planets with the Sun were at their highest position, Queen Kausalya gave birth to a son with lotus-eyes, rose-coloured lips, face like the full moon, and dark brown complexion. He, who was adored by all the worlds and the greatly blessed epitome of Vishnu, was named Rama.

The kingdom and the new father were ecstatic. They finally had an heir. Soon after, King Dasharatha's other two wives also gave birth. Bharat was born of Kaikeyi and Sumitra gave birth to twins—Lakshmana and Shatrughna. The Ikshvaku clan now had four able heirs. King Dasharatha's fears were allayed. There would be a worthy succession for his kingdom.

"Was Ravana aware of the birth of Lord Vishnu as the prince of Ayodhya, Lord?" Draupadi asked.

"King Dasharatha had relationships with many kings around the world. When his four princes were born, the elated king dispatched messengers to the ends of the earth to announce his blessed tidings. Eventually, word reached Ravana in Lanka too. Ravana congratulated the king and sent Dasharatha many precious gifts including the *Ravana Samhita*, a book on Hindu astrology, and the *Arka Prakasham*, a book on *Siddha* (spiritual medicine and treatment) for the princes' education."

"Did Ravana write those books himself, Mahadev?"

"Yes, Ravana was also an author and wrote several books over his lifetime. These two were the most important ones."

"There is absolutely nothing this man could not do," Draupadi said, incredulously.

Mahadev grinned. "No, there was not."

The royal messenger walked through the hallway en route the court where King Dasharatha was holding court. Upon being presented, the messenger bowed to the king and addressed him.

"O great king, I come from the land of Mithila where the wise King Janaka rules," the messenger stated.

"I know of your prudent king and your land, O *doot* (royal messenger)," the king said. "Tell me what news of King Janaka and his land, Mithila?"

"The king sends you his warmest greetings and wishes to let you know of his eldest daughter's swayamvara. For King Janaka's daughter, Sita, has grown up to be a fierce warrior, well versed in all the Vedas and the *shastras* (all the scriptures). She is also a woman of unparalleled beauty and charm. Devi Sita will make a great wife to an extremely fortunate man. The King of Mithila wishes to invite your eldest son, Rama to her swayamvara, O King Dasharatha," the messenger said.

"This is great news, indeed. Please pass my deepest congratulations to the king on this incredibly special occasion, O royal messenger, and let him know that my son Rama, will be honoured to attend," King Dasharatha replied.

King Janaka surveyed the hall set up for the swayamvara with special attention to the table holding the Pinaka. While his heart shuddered with fear, his mind was made up that only the person who could lift the bow would marry his daughter, Sita. The king hoped there could be found a worthy warrior amidst all the exceptional guests he had invited.

Satisfied with the arrangements, King Janaka went to pay his respects to Devi Gargi, Sita's teacher.

"What is the significance of the Pinaka bow, my Lord?" Draupadi asked.

Mahadev smirked.

"The Pinaka bow belongs to me," the Lord replied. "I gave it to King Janaka's forefather, Devrata, after being pleased with his deep worship and abiding faith in me. The king of Mithila staged his daughter Sita's swayamvara with the condition that only the person who can lift the bow will marry his daughter."

"Is the Pinaka difficult to lift?" Draupadi asked.

"The Pinaka cannot be lifted by mortals except the ancestors of Devrata who came to the throne. The only other mortal who has lifted the bow is Devi Sita. Many years ago, one day when she was only a child, Sita while playing easily lifted the table upon which the Pinaka was placed. King Janaka happened to be in the room and was aghast at his daughter's ability. Since that day, he was determined to find his daughter a husband who could at least be her equal."

"But, Devi Sita is no ordinary woman, my Lord. She is Goddess Lakshmi incarnate. So, this would imply that only the Tridev and the Tridevi can lift the Pinaka," Draupadi inferred.

"You are right, O queen," Mahadev smiled. "Only the Tridev and the Tridevi can lift the Pinaka."

"And, so, Lord Rama lifted the bow and married Devi Sita."

"He did not just lift the bow, he broke it," Mahadev corrected the queen.

King Dasharatha's joy knew no bounds. Not only were his sons married to the foremost women in the land, but he had also now proclaimed Rama to be his successor. For Rama had married the princess of Mithila, Sita, with great pomp and glory while Lakshmana wed Sita's younger sister, Urmila. Bharat, meanwhile, married Janaka's younger brother, Khushadwaja's eldest daughter Mandavi and Shatrughna wed Khushadwaja's younger daughter, Shrutakirti. The kingdom was rejoicing in the royal family's happiness. It was the most festive time for the land of Ayodhya. The kingdom shone with jubilation and glee.

"Oh, if it were not for Kaikeyi and her evil nature, Ayodhya would not have experienced its grim history, my Lord," Draupadi said with sorrow.

"Kaikeyi was not evil, Draupadi. She lost everything including how history would remember her for what she did," the Lord replied.

"She deserved it though, did she not?"

"She did not, and you will see why not," the Lord said.

Kaikeyi was joyous. Ayodhya had the worthiest successor of any kingdom in the land. Rama would be the wisest and the most prudent of all kings ever to rule on Earth. Like all their subjects, Kaikeyi celebrated the day with immense fanfare and grandeur. She went to bed content and fulfilled with her husband's choice, knowing Ayodhya would be in the most commendable hands and its future secure.

As she drifted off to sleep, Kaikeyi faintly became aware of a presence in her dream, calling her towards them.

"O Maharani Kaikeyi, I have come to you today with a request."

Kaikeyi realized the presence was of none other than Lord Vishnu. Standing upright, the Lord looked resplendent, his blue body glowing with his many arms holding his conch, his Sudarshan Chakra, the lotus, and his mace.

Kaikeyi could not believe the sight before her eyes.

"I know I am dreaming. This cannot be real," the queen told herself. "This is only an illusion."

"Maharani, yes you are dreaming but this is real. I am here because I need a favour from you," Lord Vishnu responded reading the queen's thoughts.

Kaikeyi fell on her knees, prostrating herself before the Lord. "All my existence is here to do whatever you ask of me, O Lord. I am blessed to see you in this divine form today," the queen exclaimed incredulously, still unable to believe her good fortune.

"What I ask is not easy, but I come to you because no one else can help me," Vishnu said.

"Then I consider myself the luckiest person to have ever lived, my Lord. Tell me, O great Vishnu, what may I do for you?"

"The King of Ayodhya has just named Rama as his successor to the throne," the Lord began.

"He has, my Lord. We are all the more blessed for there is no one worthier than my son Rama," Kaikeyi said with joy. "He will make a great king and rule wisely."

"He will, Maharani, but that time is not now. Rama must fulfil an extremely important task before he becomes king of Ayodhya. This is why he has taken human form."

"Extremely important task? What could be more important than ruling Ayodhya, my Lord?"

"I am afraid, O queen; I cannot divulge that information yet."

"I understand. So, what would you like me to do, O Lord?" the queen asked, her mind still reeling at the Lord's words.

"Maharani, no living or divine being can change King Dasharatha's mind to name another successor, someone other than Rama. No one except you."

"But, why would I? Rama is the worthiest and the only one capable of being king, O Vishnu," Kaikeyi said. "And, who should the king name as successor in Rama's stead anyway? Who, other than Rama, in the entire kingdom has proved himself worthy enough?"

"Maharani, Rama has to fulfil the task he was born for. I have come here today to ask you to use both boons that King Dasharatha granted you all those years ago when he was fighting the great demon Shambara and you saved his life. You will use the first boon to name Bharat as the next king of Ayodhya and the second one to banish Rama to the forest."

"What? I cannot do this, O Lord. Ask me for anything else, including my life. I would consider it my good fortune to lay it at your feet. Please, do not ask this of me. I would rather die," Kaikeyi replied, her eyes full of tears.

"I know I ask a great sacrifice of you, O Kaikeyi. For if you do this, history will not remember you kindly but, no one except you can help me right now. Grant me this favour, O Kaikeyi and upon your death you shall come unto me. Go redeem both your boons from King Dasharatha and your salvation is assured."

"How many people has history misjudged, my Lord?" Draupadi asked with tears in her eyes. "Kaikeyi's sacrifice is beyond anything I could have ever thought of."

"Everything hinged upon Kaikeyi's sacrifice. Had she not done what the Lord asked of her, Rama would not be banished, Sita would not accompany him, and Ravana would never kidnap Sita. The entire universe owes Kaikeyi a huge debt of gratitude. Without her, we would not be here. You and your husbands would not be here," Mahadev replied.

"Kaikeyi is so terribly misunderstood. She is not evil. Manthara had nothing to do with Rama's exile. What a travesty this is, O Lord," Draupadi wailed. "This is wrong and has to be corrected. Kaikeyi needs to be remembered for her selfless act of pure devotion to the Lord, not denigrated for her selfishness and motherly love towards Bharat."

"This is what happens when humans are quick to judge, O queen. It is quite easy to malign someone without understanding their intentions and the reason behind their actions. We must always strive to do better to understand someone especially when we do not share their perspective," the Lord said.

"I see that now, my Lord. I see that quite clearly and repeatedly," Draupadi said, wiping her tears.

"As far as setting the record straight is concerned, remember Kaikeyi does not care much for it for upon her death she was reunited with the Supreme Being. Her selfless sacrifice and heartfelt service to the Lord, with no regard for how the present or the future would view her, made her worthy of receiving moksha."

"Yes, you are correct, Mahadev," Draupadi sighed. "And, we all know what happened next, however, I have one question, O Lord."

Mahadev nodded at Draupadi.

"What is the purpose of fourteen years? If I remember correctly, Lord Vishnu did not specify fourteen years in his appearance in Kaikeyi's dream."

"You do remember correctly, Maharani. Lord Vishnu did not specify fourteen years. In fact, He did not specify any time because He knew Kaikeyi would appropriately pick fourteen years."

"What is the story behind the fourteen years of exile, Mahadev?" the queen asked.

"Many years ago, when Lord Rama was but a student at Saptarishi Vasishtha's gurukul, the great rishi was explaining to him how to establish Ram Rajya; that is a system of government based on truth where only dharma was followed with shastras as the guiding principles and rishis and yogis as guiding lights.

For this system to be successfully established, a ruler must stay away from his kingdom for four years, must live with animals and birds and serve them happily for four years and must be in state of renunciation for six years. All of that together equals fourteen years. Rama, who had an extremely close bond with Kaikeyi, told her this upon his return from gurukul that day.

So, when the time came for Kaikeyi to choose the number of years he had to go into exile, she remembered what Rama had told her all those years ago. She also hoped in case Rama did not know what Lord Vishnu had told her, this fourteen-year period would reaffirm in him and remind him the deep abiding love Kaikeyi held for Rama. But, Rama needed no reminder. He knew all along. Which is why after that fateful day, even though everyone else avoided Kaikeyi, Rama and Sita went to her for her blessings and to thank her before leaving for their exile."

Draupadi sighed. "There seems to be always more than what meets the eye," she said half to herself.

"Indeed, there is," came Mahadev's quick reply.

The next day, Kaikeyi redeemed both her boons from King Dasharatha. Despite Dasharatha's reservations and incredible misgivings about sending his eldest son away, Rama chose exile to honour his father's word and promise. Two days later, Rama, Sita, and Lakshmana, trading in their royal robes for ochre-coloured pieces of cloth, put on the garb of ascetics and made their way into the forest.

The mood of joyful celebration that hung over the city, just a few days ago, was replaced by despondency. Unable to bear the departure of their beloved prince, the residents of Ayodhya united in their grief, gloomily trailed the chariot of Rama, Sita, and Lakshmana as the three rode further away into the forest until Rama ordered everyone to return to their homes and resume their daily lives.

The grief of separation engulfed Dasharatha who died soon after. Kaikeyi was maligned and hated by everyone. Upon his return from his travels, Bharat immediately left for the forest to try and bring Rama back to the kingdom. When Rama refused, Bharat came back with Rama's slippers. They would sit on the throne until the true king returned from his fourteen-year exile.

Rama, Sita, and Lakshmana began their forest exile in earnest. After crossing the kingdom of Koshala, the three came upon the Ganga at Sringaverapura, where a mighty canal skimmed the floodwaters of a monsoon swollen river. It is here that Rama also met his dear friend, the ruler of the original people of the land, the Nishadas, King Guha who brought to them a solidly constructed boat, that would sail well across the mighty river. Upon embarking on the boat, Rama sent his charioteer back to Ayodhya who unable to let the three go, stood on the banks of the river for as long as his eyes could continue to catch a glimpse of the royals as they sailed further away.

Once they reached the other side of the river, Rama, Sita, and Lakshmana continued their journey onward encountering several sages at Chitrakoot, including Sage Valmiki. It was also here that they met Maharishi Atri visiting Sage Valmiki, who blessed by Goddess Durga in Satya yuga, was able to receive Lord Vishnu in his avatar as Shri Rama. Rama and Lakshmana, keenly aware of the role Maharishi Atri played in their birth, paid their obeisance to him who in turn was solemnly blessed to receive a chance to wash the feet of Shri Rama and serve him a meal.

Maharishi Atri's wife Anasuya gifted Sita a sacred garland, a pious sandal paste, and a divine gem which Sita accepted with gratitude. She also gave Sita a magic ointment that could keep her looking young forever.

As the years drifted, news of the holy trinity living at Chitrakoot spread far and wide. This led Rama, Sita, and Lakshmana to leave the ashram and make their way towards the Dandakaranya forest and the Sharabhanga ashram where more hermits and yogis waited with bated breath to catch a glimpse of the divine three.

At the end of ten years, Rama, aware of what he must do next, expressed his desire to visit the ashram of Saptarishi Agastya, the older brother of their *kulguru,* Saptarishi Vasishtha. Rama knew he needed the Saptarishi's help before embarking on the next phase of their exile, where the true reason of their human birth would take form.

This visit held special significance for Rama and the Saptarishi for both knew its real purpose. Saptarishi Agastya had been waiting a long time to give Rama powerful weapons including a great bow, quivers, and a sword. The sacred bow designed by the divine architect Vishwakarma and decorated with gold and diamonds, belonged to Rama in his divine form of Lord Vishnu. The arrows, equalling the sun in their intensity and strength, were the gift of Brahma. Two quivers that never emptied of arrows and a sword along with its sheath decorated with pure gold were from Indra.

Saptarishi Agastya also taught Rama the Aditya Hridaya mantra appeasing the grace of Suryanarayana for valour and victory in all his battles.

When Rama asked for the most appropriate location to begin the next phase of their exile, Saptarishi Agastya recommended a place, at a distance of two yojanas from the ashram, atop a mountain in an ever-blooming forest valley abundant with tubers, fruits, water, and many deer. The place was called Panchavati.

Panchavati was a delight. Nestled within a grove of five banyan trees, Lakshmana built an alluring cottage where the three exiles settled comfortably. Located on the banks of the river Godavari, the cottage was surrounded by blossoming trees, inhabited by deer, peacocks, and a fascinating variety of birds. Here, many years would pass by in content with Rama, Sita, and Lakshmana involving themselves with pleasurable tasks and simple pursuits.

"This life seems so idyllic does it not, Mahadev?" Draupadi lamented knowing how the quiet would be disturbed very soon.

"It does seem idyllic but remember Maharani, Lord Vishnu, Mother Lakshmi and the Ananta did not take birth to live a peaceful, relaxing life. They did so because they were on task to fulfil their obligations and destroy evil in all its forms."

"Mahadev, I am a bit confused. You have sung many praises of Ravana but then why did Lord Vishnu take human form to kill the mighty king?"

"That is a very germane question, Maharani," replied Mahadev.

"If Ravana was so wise and just," Draupadi continued, "why did God have to take human form to kill him? In fact, why kill Ravana at all? I understand he kidnapped Sita but that, as you have said before, was pre-ordained and happened after Lord Vishnu was already incarnated as Shri Rama. What was the real reason for killing Ravana besides returning him as a gatekeeper to Vishnu?"

"Because of the inherent nature of humanity," Mahadev said, cryptically.

"Please tell me more, Mahadev," the queen implored.

"When someone takes human form, no matter how divine they are, they struggle with their humanity. That is the intended result of the exercise. They experience human emotions of happiness, sadness, anger, disgust, fear, and so on. They struggle with their *ahamkara* and look for varied ways to satisfy it. To a lesser degree, it happened to both Lord Krishna and to Lord Rama.

Sometimes their 'good' side wins, other times the 'bad' side overtakes. With time, experience at being human determines which side surpasses at the expense of another. That does not mean someone who does many bad deeds is incapable of doing good ones and vice versa. It just means with experience, you either decide you want to work towards performing good deeds more often or want to involve yourself in tasks that lead to your personal selfish satisfaction."

Draupadi nodded in acknowledgment.

"So, coming back to Ravana. Being a gatekeeper of Vishnu in Vaikuntha meant he was inherently divine. However, as Ravana of Lanka he was human, consequently subject to all the travails of being human. He was educated, learned, and was exceptionally intelligent but he was also a king with a huge army and an extremely well-equipped navy, which meant he had a lot of power.

Over time, Ravana conquered many new territories, kingdoms and annexed his rule to faraway lands. Not many kings could stand in the way of Ravana's brilliant acumen and might. Much of this success made his human form arrogant, haughty, and egotistical. It started to think of Ravana as greater than any living being, god or asura. He was enormously powerful indeed, but Ravana became blind to his power and started using it for his own satisfaction opposed to worldly good. He began ignoring good, benevolent advice, seeking the path of destruction and annihilation to get more. But, the problem was there was no limit to more. There was always more to be had: more desire, more ambition, more greed, more of everything. Because, more was never enough.

On the spectrum of humanity, this is the farthest side of being human; a trait that will become especially common in humans during the Kali yuga. As time goes on, humans will eventually exploit everything, plunder the planet, ruin the Earth, trample those who stand in their way, exterminate the weak and vulnerable and disregard every path of *dharma* (law) in their quest for more. More money, more power, more control, more of everything until eventually Lord Vishnu will have to descend again to destroy evil once more," Mahadev said, his face fiery.

Draupadi trembled at his words. She was afraid not only for the future of her family and her clan but also for humans overall. The queen shuddered to think of humanity's end of days. If they would be anything like Dwarka's, they would be intensely barbaric and brutal. She could not imagine a world that would need to meet such a ruthless end. But, that is what Mahadev was telling her the world would be reduced to and ultimately deserve.

"Over the course of Ravana's long rule, he changed," Mahadev continued bringing Draupadi back from her vision of the apocalypse. "There was no precise moment to pinpoint the change but over time the power went to his head and he became a megalomaniac. In a way it had to happen because his time was up, and he was needed back at Lord Vishnu's door. Everything, as it always does, had to come full circle. Because of the enormity of the sheer supremacy Ravana yielded, though, no normal human or *deva* could kill him. So, the Gods went to Lord Vishnu who recognized that he had to free his old guard from his mortal form," Mahadev said.

"Everything always comes full circle," Draupadi said repeating Mahadev, slowly emphasizing the importance of each word in her mind.

"At all times. It is the cyclical nature of every law this universe fundamentally abides by."

"Mahadev, you said both Lord Krishna and Lord Rama struggled in their human form. How is that?"

"Let us talk about Lord Krishna's struggles another time," Mahadev said a small grin forming on his face. "As far as Lord Rama is concerned, let us return to Panchavati so you can see for yourself."

It was an early winter morning. The trio had just returned from the Godavari river after performing their morning ablutions. Sita entered the cottage to prepare some breakfast while Ram and Lakshmana arranged the firewood at the front of their home.

"Brother, your favourite autumn season has set in. Although the dew is harsh to the body and water is unenjoyable, fire is so delightful right now. Somehow my mind travels to Ayodhya and to our brother Bharat. I wonder how he is keeping."

At Bharat's mention, Rama smiled. He missed Bharat and his tales. Rama wondered too this morning how Bharat was doing, how Mother Kaikeyi was doing, how all of Ayodhya was doing.

Lakshmana continued. "I feel so much love for our brother although he was born to a mother who does not deserve any respect from us."

"Stop it, Lakshmana," Rama admonished his younger brother, his voice rising. "It is a sin to talk such about any mother but especially so about one of ours. Mother Kaikeyi loves us three as much as she loves Bharat. Sometimes people do things for reasons that are not easily obvious to us but rest in the knowledge that there exists a greater purpose for Mother Kaikeyi's actions," Rama explained, his voice softening.

An embarrassed Lakshmana apologized to his brother. "Sometimes such perspective is easy to forget, brother. I am sorry for my disrespectful words."

"It is, yet you must try and do better," Rama advised.

After a breakfast of wild berries, grapes, and guavas, the three rested at the front of their home in the cool fall breeze. Tonight would be a good night to light a fire.

Rama reminded his younger brother to fetch more wood from the forest.

"I shall head over right away, brother," Lakshmana said getting up.

As he started to walk out of the cottage and into the pathway leading to the forest, Lakshmana noticed someone walking towards him. A woman with elongated, gorgeous, fish-shaped, brown eyes, a slim body and thick, long, brown hair strode up the path towards their cottage. Singing a soft tune, Lakshmana could hear her mellifluous voice. His heart lurched as he stared at this strange woman whose beauty could bewitch any *deva* from *Swarga Loka*.

"O enchanted woman, who are you and what are you doing here all alone?" Lakshmana asked her.

"I was named Minakshi at birth, although everyone now calls me Surpankha. I was walking through the forest and got lost. Could you give me some water to quench my thirst so I can be on my way after?" Surpankha replied.

"I most certainly can, Devi," Lakshmana responded. "Walk with me to the door where my brother Rama and his wife Sita sit."

The two walked to the edge of the cottage door when Surpankha's eyes fell on the couple. Looking at Rama's broad shoulders, his mighty arms, conch-shaped neck, and coppery eyes that shone with kindness, Surpankha was mesmerized. His glossy face gleamed with a dark-brown complexion showing off his well chiselled features taking Surpankha's breath away.

"You are divinity in human form," she told him. "Please tell me who you are for I have fallen hopelessly in love with you."

"O Devi, my name is Rama, and this is my wife Sita," Rama said pointing to Sita who bowed to Surpankha. Surpankha noticed his deep voice sounded like the hum of a kettledrum.

"I do not care that you have a wife, O Rama," she said, dismissing Sita's greeting. "Marry me and make me whole again. I have not known love for so long since my husband left for *Swarga Loka*. I pray to you, O Rama, marry me so I can feel what it is like to be loved and cherished again," Surpankha insisted.

"O Devi, you flatter me with your kind words, but I cannot marry you or anyone else. I am married to Sita and will stay completely devoted to her for the rest of our lives. My brother, Lakshmana though," said Rama smilingly, "may be willing to take another wife. Why don't you ask him?"

"I do not love Lakshmana; I love you, O Rama. Marry me," she pleaded again.

Sita started to get uncomfortable. "O Devi," she said. "There is no one here who can marry you. Pray drink your water and leave us so we can be in peace."

"Oh, she is not bothering us, dear wife," Rama said to Sita. "Surpankha, go ask Lakshmana if he will marry you. He may just agree to for no one can doubt that you are a beautiful and enchanting woman."

"Husband, do not play with her feelings," Sita urged. "Devi, I request you to please leave before something happens that we all regret," Sita pleaded with Surpankha.

Lakshmana, standing by the front door of the cottage now joined the others. "No, brother, I would not want to marry her either. She is undoubtedly beautiful, but her nose is slightly crooked, and those ears stick out just a little. Once we fix those, she may be worthy for someone but if she is not good for you, I cannot marry her either."

The two brothers bantered back and forth for a few more minutes ignoring Surpankha who was getting angrier with each word.

"Enough!" Surpankha thundered, her voice raging, her lips trembling, tears forming in her eyes. "I, a widow, come to you with love and give you myself wholly and this is how you treat me?" she said addressing Rama. "Is this righteous behaviour from both of you? You should both know to do better. Do you know who I am and the devastation I can reign on you? How dare you presume to pass me around amongst yourselves like I am some toy? I am no plaything, let me show you what I can do," Surpankha suddenly lurched towards Sita trying to claw the queen with her long nails.

Lakshmana, quick to react, jumped up with his knife and pulled Surpankha back towards the edge of the door. Throwing her out, he raged, beside himself with anger, his wrath knowing no bounds as he walked menacingly towards Surpankha.

"You touched my sister-in-law? The woman who is purest of the pure? How dare you touch her?" Lifting Surpankha by her neck, as she struggled to breathe, her legs waving in midair, Lakshmana brought her closer to him and inched the knife next to her face.

"I would love to see what you can do now," he said mockingly to Surpankha. "You are a rotten woman who thinks she is beautiful. Is this the face you are proud of?" he said running the edge of the knife on Surpankha's cheek. "Let me see how proud you are of your face now," said Lakshmana, swiftly cutting off her nose and both her ears with his sharp knife and threw her on the ground.

Surpankha cried out, wailing in pain, her screams reverberating through the forest. Animals took cover, birds sought the safety of their nests in broad daylight for *prakriti* (nature) could sense the far-reaching aftershocks of this catastrophic attack.

Inside the cottage, Sita stared at Surpankha and Lakshmana in disbelief. She could not comprehend this sudden escalation of events. Rama stood beside her silently watching Lakshmana assault an unarmed, helpless woman. Hearing Surpankha's welp of pain, Rama simply sighed and entered the cottage.

The events had been set in motion. There was simply no turning back. Rama's humanity struggled with the enormity of the task his divinity knew would be no trouble achieving.

"So, the path to Ravana lay with Surpankha," Draupadi heaved a sigh. "I get that, but it is still unfair to mistreat a woman like this," Draupadi said to Mahadev, resigned. "I cannot believe Shri Rama let such injustice take place right under his nose."

"No matter the time: Dwapara yuga or Treta yuga," the queen thought to herself, "Women cannot find a way to be treated with respect. Wonder when that will change."

"Indeed, it is unfair. Remember the nature of humanity, Maharani? That is what is at display here. Shri Rama could have stopped the mistreatment of Surpankha but then the chain reaction that was set off would not have been. Besides, he knew Surpankha was at his cottage with her own motive," Mahadev responded.

"What motive did she have?" Draupadi asked, still irked with the treatment meted out to Surpankha.

"Do you think that Surpankha genuinely wanted to be Rama's wife? She was taken by him no doubt, for who could resist Rama's radiance, but Surpankha knew who Rama was; he had after all killed her grandmother Tadaka and her uncle Subahu, both immensely powerful and brave warriors. Surpankha knew only Rama could kill Ravana so she needed an excuse to engage Ravana with Rama."

"Excuse to engage Ravana with Rama? But, why would she want to kill her own brother?" Draupadi asked in rising disbelief.

"Many years ago, Surpankha secretly married the prince of the Kalkeya clan, Vidyutjihva. The clan and Ravana were mortal enemies of each other. When Ravana found out, he flew in a fit of rage but calmed down after his wife, Mandodari's insistence. Over time, he accepted the marriage and eventually Vidyutjihva and Ravana became allies. One day, while in battle to conquer the underworld, Vidyutjihva, who still hated Ravana but played his friend to gain his trust, tried to kill him. Ravana, acting in self-defence, murdered his sister's husband.

Suprankha was beside herself with grief. When Ravana tried explaining what happened, she would not believe him, instead blaming her brother for pretending to like Vidyutjihva all this time so he could kill him at the opportune moment. Since then, she was thirsting for her brother's death. Aware of Rama's sheer prowess, Surpankha knew she now had the opportunity for revenge she so desperately sought.

After Lakshmana cut off her ears and nose, Surpankha wailed to Ravana to avenge her insult and assault. We all know what happened next," Mahadev said.

"Yes," Draupadi sighed. "We do."

"There is, though, one pivotal thing we must see before Mother Sita is kidnapped. Let us return to Panchavati."

Two days after the Surpankha incident, early morning after their ablutions, Lakshmana went to the forest to chop wood. Rama and Sita lingered in the cottage, Sita preparing a garland while Rama cleaned his weapons.

"Sita," Rama called her gently, his voice brimming with love for his wife.

"Yes, my dear," Sita responded coming closer to her husband.

The past two days had been exceedingly difficult for the couple. The memory of the gruesome violence was only exacerbated by their knowledge of what they knew was to come next. The path would be difficult to traverse yet Rama and Sita knew it could not be avoided.

"The time for which we took human form is finally here," Rama said with sadness in his voice. "We must prepare for the event. Are you ready?"

Sita nodded hesitantly, the pain in her heart springing forth. "Should we do it now?" she asked her husband unhappily.

"No," Rama replied. "Tomorrow morning I will send Lakshmana on a longer errand. While he is away, we shall perform the ritual. Tonight, will be our last night together for a while."

"What *yagna* are they performing, Mahadev?"

"Patience, Maharani. Patience," the Lord teased Draupadi.

That night, the couple held each other tight. Tears flowed down Sita's face knowing she would not be able to cast her eyes upon the face of her beloved for a while. She would miss Rama's mighty arms that carried her, his gentle eyes that looked at her with so much love and his touch that made her delicately bronzed skin feel alive.

Rama looked at his wife's tear-streaked face and felt his heart rip apart. His love for Sita knew no limits but they were both also bound by the duties of their birth. Rama knew Sita would forever be his but the very thought of losing her for a while hurt him. He held her closer and kissed her smooth forehead.

"I see your pain, Sita, for it mirrors mine but worry not, my love," Rama said lovingly to his wife. "We shall be together again soon. Until then, I shall carry you in my heart every minute of my existence. I love you more than I can bear but we must do what we are born for."

"I know, my beloved," Sita responded her face dry with tears. "We must and we will. We will carry forth our obligations. I look forward to the day when I shall see you again and be held in these mighty arms once more." Arm in arm the couple fell asleep waiting for the morning sun's rays to commence the first undertaking tied to the reason for their birth.

Early in the morning, Rama sent Lakshmana on an errand to Saptarishi Agastya's ashram. As soon as he left, the divine couple got started.

Seated in front of the holy fire, Shri Rama summoned Lord Agni. Immediately, the ruddy figure of Agni Deva began to appear.

"My Lord, tell me what I must do," Lord Agni asked Rama.

"The time has come, Lord Agni. I have beckoned you here to perform the switch to keep Sita away."

"I am ready, my Lord," he said. "Mother Sita, I offer you my greetings. Shall we begin?" Agni asked Sita.

Sita nodded. "Yes, we shall, Lord Agni. Tell me what to do."

"Slowly enter the pit, Mother Sita, so I may wrap my cloak around you to keep you safe. Once that is done, we shall proceed with replacing your presence."

Sita cast one last look at Rama. With abiding love in his eyes, Rama took her hands and kissed them. "I love you," he mouthed the words slowly. As her tears began to flow again, Sita smiling tenderly through them walked into Lord Agni's fire and disappeared.

A few seconds later, Lord Agni returned. "It is done, my Lord. Mother Sita is situated and safe. Shall we begin with the next phase?"

"Yes," Rama responded his voice sad.

Gradually, the fire started to burn brighter. Next to Lord Agni stood another figure of a woman with a sculpted bronze body, thin waist, shining black hair, and a full bosom. Her face shone with the softness of the moonlight, her iridescent eyes hiding behind her long and velvety eye lashes.

Folding her hands, she bowed to Shri Rama. "Your humble servant offers you my prayers, my Lord. I thank you for calling upon me in your time of need."

Rama smiled and bowed in return. Although the figure emanating from the fire resembled his wife, Sita, he knew it was not her. "A brother can only think to call upon his sister during dire times. I dare not call anyone else, O Chaya. I thank you for answering my plea."

Chaya Sita then emerged from the fire and took the place, normally occupied by Sita, next to Rama.

"Is there anything else I can help with, my Lord?" Lord Agni asked.

"There is not. I thank you for your help."

Lord Agni bowed to Rama and disappeared into the fading fire.

"Where did Lord Agni take Mother Sita, Mahadev?"

"He took her to the seat vacated by Chaya, where Parvati sits."

"Wouldn't that be Mount Kailash with you?"

Mahadev nodded in agreement.

"Is that why Shri Rama called Chaya his sister? Because, in essence she is Mother Parvati?"

Mahadev nodded once more. "Remember, there is an *ansh* (aspect) of Devi Sati in the fire. This is the *ansh* that was born as Vedavati and came back as Chaya Sita during Treta yuga. Sati is Parvati incarnate, who is the sister of Lord Vishnu. Lord Rama was merely recalling the relationship the two of them share."

"I see," Draupadi nodded. "I understand now. So, Chaya, who is also Vedavati, is here with Rama to become the cause of Ravana's death."

"Yes, Mother Sita or Lord Rama could kill Ravana all on their own if they wanted. But, in making this switch, they made it possible to obtain Ravana's approval since, you may recall, he was the one who suggested to Vedavati that she become the cause of his death."

"I do remember. So, does he really kidnap Chaya then? Or, does Chaya go with him willingly? I am curious to see how all that played out."

"Then let us return to Panchavati," Mahadev said.

Early next morning, Ravana arrived at Dandakaranya forest in his Pushpak *vimana*. After assessing the forest, he, and his friend Maricha, who had a boon to take any form, walked towards Panchavati. Stealthily, the two surveyed the cottage and its inhabitants. Ravana quietly noticed the trio who lived there. There were two extremely able-bodied brothers, with strong shoulders and long limbs, who looked like warriors, and a woman who was disturbingly beautiful. Ravana's heart swayed as he followed the woman's movements with his gaze. Something about her was awfully familiar but the mighty king could not pluck her identity from his memory.

Ravana and Maricha decided the best course of action lay in distracting the two men and taking the woman away. For this, they devised a plan. Maricha turned into a golden deer who the woman desired with all her heart. The man closest to her, who looked like her husband, ran to capture the deer after giving the younger man some instructions. After a while, a loud scream was heard, whereupon the woman beseeched the younger man to go after his brother and rescue him. The younger brother, torn between his duty to protect the woman and save his brother, ultimately decided to head into the forest.

Although Ravana thought all of this transpired rather quickly and easily, he knew his moment had arrived.

Few minutes after the younger brother left, dressed as a Brahmin, Ravana approached the cottage. The woman who was inside, upon hearing his cry for alms, emerged holding a bowl of rice in her hand. Ravana saw that at this distance she was even more beautiful with her perfect body, slim waist, long shiny hair, luminous eyes, and shining face. He once again noticed the familiar feeling return but still could not place her face anywhere.

"Here you are, O Brahmin. I have brought you some food," Chaya said glancing a knowing smile at Ravana.

"O beautiful one, have we met before? Why do I feel like I know you?" a perplexed Ravana asked.

Chaya smiled wider. "Of course, you know me, Ravana, as I know you. I have returned as you once asked me to."

Ravana became still. "Vedavati?" he asked her, his voice barely audibly to himself.

"Yes, it is me. Although I look like Rama's wife Sita, it is me, Vedavati. The time for your death is here now."

Despite his promise to Vedavati, Ravana was not prepared to die. "I know I promised you, alas today is not the day for me to die. I will, however, honour my promise but to do so, you must come with me."

"Come with you where?" Vedavati asked.

"To my home in Lanka. I promise to never touch you without your permission, but if you would accept my marriage proposal, I would be the most privileged of all in this world."

"I cannot marry you, Ravana, for I am here to become the cause of your death. Take me where you need to. Rama and Lakshmana will follow me and make sure you are killed."

Ravana laughed, "You shall see, Vedavati, it is not so easy to kill me. I am sure Rama and Lakshmana are very brave, but I am also King Ravana of Lanka," he said, sounding amused.

"You have changed, Ravana," Vedavati pointed out to him. "I can see your ego shining through you and perhaps this is reason enough for me to know that your time has come."

"We shall see," Ravana responded, haughtily.

The two then walked to the edge of the forest where the Pushpak *vimana* was waiting. Afterward, Ravana took Vedavati to Lanka.

Rama and Lakshmana hurriedly returned to the cottage. Even before he got back, Rama knew Chaya was gone. Lakshmana was beside himself with grief. "Where could my dear sister-in-law have gone? There are so many animals in this forest. What if one of them harmed her?" Lakshmana, not knowing the identity of Chaya, asked bellowing with sorrow.

"No harm will come upon Sita," Rama replied, his heart trembling but his voice stoic. "She will be safe, and will soon be found. Let us look around to see if we can find any clues."

Lakshmana immediately noticed a separate and bigger set of footprints alongside his sister-in-law's. He pointed them to Rama who suggested they follow them. The two brothers traced the footsteps of Ravana and Chaya to the edge of the forest where they suddenly disappeared.

"Where could this person have taken Mother Sita and how?" Lakshmana asked Rama. "How can they just disappear into thin air from here on?"

"Shri Ramaaaa," the brothers heard a shrieking cry. Looking around to locate the source of the voice, the two brothers found an injured Brahmin at the foot of a tree. Running to him Lakshmana asked, "Who did this to you?"

"It was the king of Lanka," the Brahmin replied. "I was picking berries for the ashram when I saw Mother Sita being taken into a giant flying object by King Ravana."

"Ravana?" Lakshmana said in disbelief. "What was he doing here? Are you sure you saw Mother Sita with him?"

"I would recognize Mother Sita anywhere. I am sure she was with that selfish king. When I tried to intervene, Ravana angrily jabbed me with his sword. It is also when he told me who he really was. 'You try and stop the king of Lanka, hapless Brahmin?' he said. 'Be grateful Ravana is not ending your life here today,' the king said to me. I tried to help, my Lords, but alas I could not save Mother Sita. Please forgive me, Shri Rama for I failed you."

"You failed no one, O Brahmin. Tell me your name," Rama asked him, kindly.

"My name is Jatayu, Shri Rama."

"Jatayu, I thank you for everything you did today. You are a brave man and a kind soul. We shall take you back to the ashram now where I am sure you will make a complete recovery. You have done us a great service for now we know where my wife, Sita is headed."

"Yes, Shri Rama. She is headed to Lanka with that wicked Ravana. When you capture him and release Mother Sita, please tell her I apologize for not being able to save her but thank her for saving my life from Ravana for had it not been for her intervention, that atrocious king would have surely killed me."

"I am sure Sita will be grateful that you were here today. Come now, let us take you back," Rama said.

With Lakshmana carrying Jatayu on his back the two brothers made their way towards Saptarishi Agastya's ashram.

With Jatayu safely back at the ashram, Rama and Lakshmana after receiving blessings from Saptarishi Agastya, started their long journey to Lanka. Travelling south, the two brothers eventually reached the kingdom of Kishkindha. Overnight, they decided to rest near the Pampa Lake at the foot of Mount Rishyamukha. After a small dinner, the two were ready to retire for the evening when a Brahmin approached them.

Addressing him, Rama said, "O Brahmin, we are blessed to see you, unfortunately we are travellers and have no more food left to share. If you would like, though, we can find you a meal."

The Brahmin, unusually tall with long limbs and a muscular body replied, "I do not need food, but tell me, O rishi, what are you doing here this time of night? This is a huge forest with many dangerous animals. Without proper weapons, you will become a meal for them," the Brahmin warned.

"We are two brothers traversing this route to bring my wife back," Rama replied.

"Did she leave you?" the Brahmin asked amused.

"Yes, she did," Rama replied.

"Well, maybe she does not like you then," the Brahmin joked.

The thought of Sita not liking him brought a sad smile to Rama's lips. "She was taken away forcibly," he said.

"What? Who would do such a ghastly thing?"

"I am Rama, and this is my brother, Lakshmana. My wife, Sita, was taken away by King Ravana of Lanka. My brother and I are headed there to rescue her," Rama said.

The Brahmin suddenly fell to Rama's feet.

"My Lord, forgive me, your most humble servant, for it took me so long to recognize you."

"Get up, Brahmin. Who are you and why are you asking for my forgiveness?" Rama asked.

The Brahmin wiped tears of joy running down his face. "You are Shri Rama; my Lord Rama, and I am Hanuman, your biggest devotee." Saying this, the Brahmin was replaced by the mighty valorous monkey, of terrific deeds, with his body as strong as a diamond, the golden mace shining in his hand.

Rama's eyes shone with delight. "Hanuman, I am so glad to have found you. I need to find Sita. Will you help me?"

"I will do anything for you, my Lord, but let me first take you to King Sugriva who hides in this mountain, afraid of his brother Vali. I am sure he and his army will help you find Mother Sita. Let us make haste."

"Maharani, do you know how Lord Krishna died?" Mahadev asked Draupadi.

Her friend's name brought fresh pain to her heart. Draupadi, who had not for one moment forgotten Krishna was dead, felt riled up again at Mahadev's words. Achingly she responded, "I do not, Mahadev."

"Sugriva's brother Vali was an enormously powerful monkey who had defeated many great kings. He was such an embodiment of strength that when challenged by Ravana, he tied him around his tail and spun him around the world until the King of Lanka accepted defeat."

"Vali did that to Ravana?" an amused Draupadi asked. The thought of anyone treating Ravana in this manner was now exceedingly difficult for the queen to accept.

"Yes, one of the only kings who defeated Ravana, Vali was the ruler of Kishkindha. When Sugriva decided to help Rama in his search for Sita, Rama in exchange agreed to defeat Vali and crown Sugriva as king. When Sugriva and Vali were fighting, Rama could not identify which brother was which and so the next time they met, Sugriva wore a special garland to be distinguished from his very alike older brother. Rama thus knew who Vali was and shot an arrow from his hiding place to kill the great king.

Upon receiving his death from Shri Rama, Vali, who was highly learned and educated, addressed the human form of Lord Vishnu, "My dear Lord, lives I will get many, but a death like this when will I get again. To die in Your presence is the greatest fortune and it is a perfection of life. I seek only that I can behold your face and die in your presence."

Vali then gave his necklace, a source of his immeasurable power and invincibility, to his younger brother Sugriva, whom Vali now realized he had greatly misunderstood.

In this sense, Rama used *chhal* to defeat and kill Vali. Rama also killed Vali by shooting an arrow in his back. Rama knew what he did was wrong but since there was no alternative, he had to proceed with this deception. This is yet another example of the divine doing what humans do because that is the intended outcome of the experience."

Draupadi understood. She nodded.

"The universe, however, was imbalanced since Rama owed Vali," Mahadev continued. "So, later when Shri Rama came back as Shri Krishna, Jara the hunter, who was really Vali from Treta yuga, released an arrow that killed Keshav when he was resting under the banyan tree outside Somnath. With the death of Krishna at Jara's hands, the balance was now corrected."

Draupadi's eyes were clouded with tears. "So, Krishna knew all along. Of course, he knew all along. Why did he not tell me?"

"He could not tell you, Maharani. It was for him to do and for you to find out here today. Rama killed Vali and Jara killed Krishna. That is the cyclical nature of this universe, the debt that was owed was now paid," Mahadev explained.

Draupadi sobbed softly.

"Once Vali was dead," Mahadev continued, "King Sugriva was crowned king of Kishkindha. To fulfil his end of the bargain, the king gathered a massive army to find Mother Sita in Lanka. But, before they could march there, the monkey king needed confirmation that Sita was indeed in Lanka. For this, he turned to his most trusted lieutenant, Hanuman. After being reminded by Jambavan the bear, that he could fly, Hanuman took a giant leap over the sea, into the skies and flew in the direction of Lanka to find Shri Rama's wife."

After battling several sea monsters and numerous threats along the way, Hanuman finally reached Lanka. He was amazed to see the prosperity of the city. Lined in gold, Lanka shone with a radiance Hanuman had never seen before. Rejoiced and happy, the inhabitants abounded Lanka's city lanes, buying and selling goods with affluence. Full of elephants, horses, and chariots, the city had four massive gates fitted with strong doors and huge beams for locking them. A great wall made of gold, decorated at intervals with gems, corals, cat's eyes, and pearls encircled the entire city forming an impenetrable fortress.

Lanka looked impregnable, an ethereal stronghold surrounded by water, built on a mountain its defences included a forest as well as abundant artificial fortification. Hanuman paused wondering how Rama and the army would ever succeed in breaching Lanka's walls.

Hanuman searched the length and breadth of Lanka for Mother Sita. After what seemed an eternity, he finally found her at Ashoka Vatika, a gorgeous garden surrounded by Ashoka trees and their delicate cerise flowers, guarded, and tended by Lankan maids. Although Mother Sita was safe and looked unharmed, Hanuman noticed she was extremely emaciated. Lonely and despondent, her radiance beaming through her, Mother Sita sat unbathed under an Ashoka tree, making a garland, patiently waiting for the day her captivity would end.

After meticulously making his approach, careful not to alert her guards, Hanuman introduced himself to Mother Sita as Shri Rama's envoy and produced the Lord's ring to confirm his identity.

"O Mother Sita, I am the most dedicated servant of Shri Rama and have come here to tell you the Lord is desperately waiting to see you again," Hanuman said, bowing with humility, completely unaware of the real identity of the woman who resembled Sita.

Chaya as Rama's Sita, bemoaning separation, rejoiced at Hanuman's arrival. "Is my dear husband here with you? If so, bring him to me at once so these anxious eyes can once again look upon my beloved's face," she said.

"The Lord is waiting for me with an army on the other side of the sea, Mother," Hanuman replied, his hands folded in prayer position. "We heard from Jatayu that Ravana abducted you but before we would march in here with an army, we needed irreversible proof that you were indeed here in Lanka. Now that I have found you, you can come with me back to the Lord."

With sadness in her eyes, Chaya said, "I cannot, Hanuman. I am extremely pleased that you have found me because now Rama and Lakshmana will know to come and free me. Alas, I cannot come with you."

"Why not, Mother? I can make sure you are comfortable and take you back safely."

"I am not concerned about my safety or comfort, Hanuman. I know I will forever be safe with you. But, I cannot escape like this. I want to be freed with respect instead of escaping in the dead of the night."

Hanuman nodded. He understood and respected Sita's wishes. He also knew he would not be able to change her mind. He would go back to Lord Rama and tell him all about his meeting with Mother Sita.

"There is one thing though I wish for you to tell my beloved husband," Chaya said.

"Anything you wish, Mother. Just say the words. I shall make sure Lord Rama hears them in their entirety," Hanuman said, his eyes brimming with devotion and elation.

"Give him this," Chaya handed Hanuman the divine gem Anasuya had given Sita, "so he knows you truly found me. Tell him I am safe though my heart aches for him and tell him my days are numbered. If he does not hurry, I may not be found alive."

"Mother Sita, glorious is today for I have found you. Why do you speak such words that stab my heart with so much pain? Who would dare harm you?" Hanuman asked with pain in his heart.

Chaya smiled. "When Ravana first took me away he gave me a year to change my mind. If at the end of that period, my mind was still unchanged, he promised he would kill me. That year will be complete in a few months."

"Ravana said this to you, Mother? But, why would he kill you? What does he want from you?"

"He wants me to marry him. For this, he gave me a year to change my mind. But, what he does not understand is my mind can never be changed. I am married to Rama and I will always be."

"Mother Sita, I beg you to come along with me. It is not safe for you here," Hanuman pleaded with Chaya, acutely aware of the strength of Lanka's defences.

"I appreciate your concern for my safety, Hanuman, but I will not leave here without Rama coming to free me. Go tell Rama to make haste and come to Lanka," Chaya ordered.

Unable to change her mind, Hanuman bowed to Mother Sita and proceeded to leave Ashoka Vatika. On his way out, he was caught by Ravana's guards who brought him to their king. An enraged Ravana ordered Hanuman to be killed but his younger brother, Vibhishana, intervened advising Ravana to not engage in a cowardly act, pointing out it was against royal scriptures. For a learned Brahmin like Ravana to engage in such actions would not be graceful. Instead, Vibhishana, the convincing communicator he was, suggested setting Hanuman's tail on fire.

Ravana, convinced by Vibhishana, ordered the guards to pour oil on Hanuman's tail and set it on fire. Tying him down with ropes, the Lankan citizens unaware of Hanuman's sheer strength and tenacity, paraded him down the streets proclaiming him to be a spy. After letting them have their fun, Hanuman finally decided to take matters in his own hands. Using his powers, Hanuman enlarged himself now bigger than any mountain and then immediately shrunk back to the size of a mouse to escape his captors. With his tail ablaze, the powerful monkey flew over Lanka, setting the entire city on fire. Leaving a trail of flames throughout, Hanuman, the son of Vayu, the god of wind, then dipped his tail into the sea and leapt back to Rama to convey the happy news that his wife was found, and she was secure.

Overjoyed at the news, Rama started to immediately prepare to march on Lanka. There was, however, a crucial problem. A vast sea stood before Rama's army and Ravana's Lanka. How to cross it posed a critical question which if not answered would end all talk of conquest before it even began. To resolve it, Rama started to invoke the god of the ocean, Lord Varuna. Upon appearance, Lord Varuna told Rama the bridge could not be built because the king of Lanka was under the protection of Lord Shiva who also considered Ravana his biggest devotee. Until this protection was removed by Lord Shiva himself, there would be no way forward for Rama and the monkey army.

"This is quite the quandary now for Shri Rama," Draupadi observed.

"It indeed is, for not just the bridge could not be built without my blessing but also the fastest way to reach me is through my biggest devotee who in Treta yuga was King Ravana," Mahadev said.

"So, what happened then?"

"Well, Sage Narada just happened to be in the area. When Shri Rama told him his dilemma, Narada suggested Rama send him, as his envoy, to Lanka to ask Ravana to perform a ritual for me so I could bless their venture," Mahadev replied.

"Sage Narada never just happens to be anywhere," Draupadi said, laughing heartily. "And, why would Ravana perform the ritual when he knows its purpose is only to harm him?"

"Ravana knew the purpose of the ritual yet he still performed it."

"He did!" Draupadi, her eyes wide with disbelief, responded to Mahadev.

"He did and that, Maharani, is the greatness of Ravana," Mahadev said. "Ravana knew I would respond immediately once he invoked me and grant permission to the army to build a bridge to Lanka. He knew the purpose of the bridge and he knew what Rama intended to do once he and his army got there. Despite all this knowledge, he as my biggest devotee, performed the yagna for Rama for he could not refuse anyone my worship. Thereafter, he returned to Lanka to wait for his end. With Vedavati born again and Rama having received my blessing, Ravana knew the time of his death was upon him. But, being the warrior he was, Ravana did not give up without a fight."

"But, ultimately he did die."

"Yes," Mahadev nodded, "as all humans must, Ravana died. He was mortally wounded by the extremely powerful weapon of Brahma, the *Brahmastra,* given to Rama by Saptarishi Agastya. But, before he died, upon Rama's suggestion, Ravana imparted invaluable knowledge about the *shastras* and running a kingdom to Lakshmana. Ravana was a great human, a mighty warrior, a just king, and an extremely educated Maha-Brahman. Men like him do not grace the Earth often. Although his end was needed, Earth lost a valuable leader that day," Mahadev said, pensively.

With the death of King Ravana, Rama and his army were victorious. Lanka saw a great deal of loss of life and although the kingdom and its inhabitants were extremely sad on losing their great king, they saw the divinity of Rama and accepted his rule. Rama, on the other hand, had no intention of ruling Lanka and immediately established Vibhishana, Ravana's younger brother, as the ruler. Before that though, Mother Sita had to be freed from Ashoka Vatika.

Rama went to the garden to see his beloved wife. Upon seeing each other, the royal couple's joy knew no bounds. Rama rushed towards Chaya to embrace her, grateful for her safety before Chaya stopped him in his tracks.

Continuing the charade for everyone else who thought she was Sita, Chaya said to Rama, "Do not take another step closer to me, my dear husband. Although I crave to embrace you, I must first cleanse myself with the holy fire."

Without another word, Chaya sat on the ground in a meditative pose to invoke Lord Agni. Lord Agni, expecting a summon any minute, immediately appeared, while Rama along with his retinue and the guards in the garden watched, awestruck by Sita's actions.

"O Agni Deva, admit me within your flames so I may clean myself before embracing my husband." Agni Deva obliged.

Chaya glanced at Rama. "I will see you soon," he said to her.

Confused at Rama's words, Chaya entered the red flames protected by Agni Deva. A few seconds later, Mother Sita emerged from the fire and ran to her husband who embraced his wife with utmost vigour. Rama and Sita were reunited.

Draupadi smiled.

"It is good to see Rama and Sita together again, is it not?" Mahadev asked Draupadi.

The queen nodded. "Yes, I am happy to see Rama and Sita reunited, Mahadev. But, I am also confused at Shri Rama's words."

"You mean when he said he would see you soon?" Mahadev asked.

"Yes, exactly those. I think I may know the reason for them," Draupadi said, realization dawning on her slowly. "So, Mahadev, in Shri Rama's life Chaya was the presence of Mother Parvati."

"You are right, O queen."

"Mother Sarasvati told me that according to a curse on Lord Vishnu, he cannot return to Vaikuntha and be completely free from the shackles of his human form until Mother Kali blesses his mortal coils. I blessed Krishna's mortal coils so he could be released. Did Shri Rama say those words to Chaya because she was recalled at the time of his death?"

"That is indeed the case, Maharani. Before he drowned in the Sarayu, Shri Rama invoked Agni and called you once more to help him. That is when he also made you a promise."

"What promise?"

"Let us go find out."

On the banks of the river Sarayu, King Rama, having handed control of his kingdom to his sons Lauv and Kush, invoked Agni Deva once again. It was time for Rama to depart Earth. Mother Sita and Lakshmana, both having given up their human forms, were waiting for Vishnu in Vaikuntha. Rama was ready but he needed help with one final task.

"O Agni Deva, I need your and Chaya's help once more," Rama said to the god of fire.

"We are here to help you, my Lord," Agni Deva said. Chaya walked out of the fire.

"I see that I *do* see you again," Chaya said to Rama, a smile on her lips.

"Dear sister, I need your help one last time in this birth," Rama said.

"Yes, I know," Chaya replied. "I will bless your mortal coils once you give up your human form."

"I thank you for all the help and sacrifice you have provided me, Chaya. We did not get much time to spend together in this lifetime, but I promise we will do so as dear friends in the future."

Chaya smiled. "I will look forward to it."

Bowing to each other, Chaya stood by the banks of the Sarayu river as Rama blessed all of nature and took his last breath in this lifetime.

Draupadi smiled too, her memories of Krishna and their time together flashing before her eyes. Her friend, Krishna, gave her a promise and he kept it. Not only did he spend time together with her, but he also gave her invaluable advice and help on so many things. For who but Keshav would guide her lonely existence, console her in her hopeless grief, visit her during those endless nights she spent crying herself to sleep, tell her tales of this world until she dozed off. Without him, she would not know how to live out her exile, how to feed anyone who came to her home unannounced, how to calm her raging inferno, how to handle her husbands' unique personality and so much more!

Draupadi could not count the innumerable ways Krishna had enriched her life, enhanced her existence, and showed up at her doorstep whenever she needed him carrying the queen through her most difficult times.

The queen could never fathom how he could have done all of that but now she knew it was because he was the Supreme Truth of the universe.

The queen remembered the time she and Krishna spent together, the laughter they shared, the tears she shed when she was sad but how Krishna was always there for her. She missed him dearly for she knew he would never return, and she would never see him again in his playful form. But, her heart held on to all his memories, and Draupadi basked in the knowledge that she could reminisce about Krishna whenever she so desired.

Draupadi felt special, she felt chosen. For this, she owed Krishna a debt she knew she would never be able to pay back. For her life, although difficult and extremely complicated at times, was made easier by her friend and now she recognized, her brother; although to her their bond went well beyond all those material words.

Still hurt at all her losses, the queen's heart ached but for the first time since the great war, Draupadi felt calm. Her fire, dare she say, was slowly fading leaving her alive with the knowledge of her true being. The information being revealed to her was serving as a great antidote to the agitation the queen had felt for almost her entire life. Draupadi, for the first time, was starting to understand and embrace her divine self.

Mahadev smiled to himself, gratified with Draupadi's progress and her assertion. He was beginning to see the change and the manifestation in the queen. The raging queen was slowly but surely being replaced by her true divine form, the quintessential shakti of the universe. Mahadev's joy knew no bounds.

He knew there would be no turning back.

Part IV

Nalayani

We worship the three-eyed One, who is fragrant and who nourishes all.

Like the fruit falls off from the bondage of the stem, may we be liberated from death, from mortality.

—*Maha Mrityunjaya Mantra* for Lord Shiva, usually chanted 108 times

~ The numbers 1, 0, and 8 signify 'oneness', 'nothingness', and 'everything' respectively. Together the numbers show the ultimate truth that the universe is one, empty and infinite all at once.

~ The Vedas state that the distance between the Sun and the Earth and the Earth and the Moon is 108 times the diameter of the Sun and the Moon, respectively.

~ There are 108 Upanishads.

5

Mahadev noticed the queen was unusually quiet. She looked composed although Mahadev could tell she was overwhelmed. The Lord understood. Draupadi had shown remarkable magnanimity so far. Not many devas could demonstrate the chivalry the queen had exhibited in such extraordinary circumstances. Draupadi, though, was only a mortal. Divinity but mortal in her current state. Mahadev could not help but admire this strong woman who was not just able to keep herself together but also continually strengthened her resolve and her equilibrium with each new revelation.

The Lord of all the Worlds knew he had made the right decision in giving Draupadi the choice to travel with him. Sure, there could have been many other ways to impart the knowledge she needed to attain her divinity, but Mahadev had chosen this route. So far, he did not regret it for Draupadi had impressed him with her inane resoluteness and sagacity. Mahadev knew about the queen's inherent nature and her poise. He was confident that despite the breadth of all the revelations, Draupadi would remain sanguine.

Draupadi did not know what to say. She felt herself different, new, perhaps unfamiliar to her own being. The queen had many questions, but she realized they did not feel as important anymore. The need for mortal urges was slowly fading away, replaced by a peace, an abiding calm within her. Draupadi had never known this part of her before. This stage, this feeling was distinct;

she did not even know it existed, for she had never travelled this far within her, to comprehend herself and calibrate her real identity. Draupadi's usual self was inexperienced to handle this changed persona, this new sense of awe and of being in control. Part of her felt scared, this territory was unconquered, it made her feel vulnerable; not exactly a comfortable place to be, the queen observed quietly.

The queen noticed she was growing in a way circumstances had never really allowed her to. Her entire life so far, as Draupadi, had been a series of responding to calamities she had no hand in creating. The queen also noticed poignantly that her birth was brought forth for the purpose of satisfying men, their extreme ambitions, and their wilful desires. She, a woman, had always been persistently careening to the whims and desires of men acting in their own self-interest.

Born from the fiery pits of Lord Agni, Draupadi came forth when she was not even called. At least that is how her father saw it. Her father, King Drupada, the ruler of Panchal, burnt with shame and was singular in his longing for vengeance from Drona, his childhood friend. As a child, Drupada studied with Drona at the ashram of Rishi Bharadwaj where the two became great friends. Over their schooling years, Drona helped the future king with many lessons, earning Drupada's irrefutable trust. Drupada then, made a promise to Drona to share half his kingdom with the brahmin. Many years later, Drupada became king and Drona lived a life of poverty.

Remembering his promise, Drona approached his old friend Drupada for help, who refused to recognize him and laughed at their childhood agreement, mocking Drona, and calling him a beggar. An infuriated Drona wanted retribution. After the military education of the Pandavas and the Kauravas, Drona asked them to capture King Drupada as his fee. Determined to give their guru his *dakshina* (fees), the Pandavas succeeded in capturing King Drupada, producing him in front of Drona who likewise derided his old friend and retained half his kingdom that Drona's students had won. Humiliated, Drupada initiated the Putrakameshti yagna for a son who would help kill the Kuru teacher. For Drupada only needed a male, Dhrishtadyumna, to avenge his insult and satisfy his hunger of Drona's death.

Draupadi was the residue, her female presence not required but eventually fully exploited to further the aspirations of her lofty father.

Fully grown, without the process of intercourse, Draupadi emerged from the fire into a world that had no sense of convention for someone as unique as her. Devoid of a childhood, the young princess of Panchal led an unusual daily life. Unlike other royal children, the princess had no friends anywhere, inside or outside the kingdom. People spoke in hushed voices when she walked by, unsure of how to conduct themselves in the presence of someone as peculiar. Draupadi was an anomaly and although she would be destined for great things, the princess heard all the quiet whispers reminding her of the aberration she knew she was.

At no time during her days in Panchal did Draupadi experience the love of her parents or any other close familial relationships. Her father, who only cared about his revenge, did not think of Draupadi as relevant or important until her wedding day when he would once again use her to create a lasting alliance for himself. She barely saw him. Her mother, Prishati, was mother in name only, choosing to be Drupad's wife and queen of Panchal above all other kinship, selecting to be completely absent in Draupadi's life. Draupadi's siblings, Dhrishtadyumna, Shikhandi, and Satyajit, were always distant clamouring for their own honour and retribution leaving Yajnaseni to spend her days without the loving presence of any human in her life. Surrounded by maids and courtiers, all of whom were slow to accept and quick to judge, the princess craved affection, hungering for a worthwhile presence amid her, all the while struggling desperately to cling onto life.

Many years passed thus with Draupadi in severe isolation with no friend or foe, no one to talk to or be outraged at. The princess muddled through her early days disoriented, with sparse knowledge of the world that existed outside her four walls.

All of that changed the day she met her dear friend. Draupadi had heard of him, talk was rife within the palace corridors about the cowherder with dark skin, like hers, who had killed his uncle Kamsa and established dharma in Mathura, visiting Panchal. She knew of his many exploits in Vrindavan, heard of how he built his city of gold in Dwarka, his unbridled passion for his many wives and his deep love for the Pandavas. Although she had never seen him before, a spark lit in the young princess the moment she lay eyes upon him. Draupadi knew him, had always known him, more than she had ever known anyone else. She could not explain this feeling, Krishna told her it need not be. Somethings were better left that way, he would say.

Draupadi could still recall the day in vivid detail, the bubbling excitement she felt when Krishna introduced himself to her, the exhilaration with which her entire being danced in his presence and the elation her heart felt knowing she mattered to him.

Krishna felt the same, he told her so. They had a bond, he explained, an equivalent connection that strung across lifetimes, one that would never dissipate but only grow more inimitable.

And so, for the first time ever, the princess of Panchal had a *sakha*; a friend she could talk to, confide in, get advice from. Someone who knew of her deep concerns, her sleepless nights and all her thoughts, who understood the immense loneliness she suffered and the many demons she battled every day. He told her she was vital, the key who would open many locks, but the princess would have to wait for her time. It would not be easy, as Draupadi would find out, but she would find his advice invaluable as the princess traversed her time on earth through her many tribulations, starting with the day of her wedding.

The day of Draupadi's swayamvara was no regular day for such an unparalleled ceremony was never witnessed before. In its preparation, for the first time since her birth from Agni's pit, the princess's father considered her although only to further his own superciliousness and pretension. For the man could not attach importance to anyone other than himself. To satisfy his pride, King Drupada invited all the mighty suitors of the land and set up a machine with a fixed golden target. The king declared, "He who can string this bow and, after stringing, shoot the target above with these arrows, will obtain my daughter." Thus, the many assembled kings of the land, brave, wealthy, and immensely powerful competed for the prize of calling the enchanting beauty, Draupadi their wife.

For there was no debate that the princess of Panchal was hauntingly gorgeous. Her dark skin tone, which earned her the name "Krishnaa" glowed with the beautiful scent of blue lotuses, deluding even the bees. Draupadi's eyes were like lotus petals, entrancing with a spirited glow, her soft, long eye lashes swaying mischievously. Her pearl like teeth, hid behind her playful smile, put lightning to shame. Draupadi's beautiful, long, curly, shining hair shimmered like the darkness of the night with her coppery nails reminiscent of the crescent moon, the princess stood tall with well swelled breasts, narrow waist, and a graceful figure.

Draupadi sat in court, all eyes upon her, while her heart sought only him. The man who encompassed everything Draupadi was looking for in a husband; the man who she knew would always respect and stand up for her. He sat amongst the assembled kings, his radiance like burning gold, his body reflecting the effulgence of the sun, with his beautiful big eyes, wide forehead, and gorgeous curly hair. Sun like resplendence, Moon like gentleness, and fire like lustre, Karna sat in the court, his lion gaze upon the target, his chest large and his shoulders broad, knowing he would win the hand of the most exceptional woman.

Alas, fate had different plans for although Karna's valour was beyond reproach and Drupada's target effortless for his skills, her father had made it known that Draupadi, the princess of Panchala, would not marry a lower caste man even though everyone could see the brightness of the sun bursting forth through him. But, that too was ignored, as were Draupadi's other dreams. She would have to go elsewhere, belong to someone else. The idea repulsed her and since that day she hated Karna partly because he chose not to fight for her.

Instead, she married a man disguised as a Brahmin who turned out to be the brave warrior Arjuna, the best archer the world had ever known. But, thanks to the word of a woman, who spoke too soon, without realizing its consequences on Draupadi, and her sons who treated Draupadi like chattel, the princess, who only married Arjuna at her swayamvara, was now to be equally divided in matrimony to five men. Five great men who sought not just mortal glory but wished to be renowned even among the gods. For they were the son of gods; the Pandavas. So, Draupadi went from being princess of Panchal to the wife of the five Pandavas, resolute in their purpose to rule and ascend to the throne at all costs. Her priorities, her feelings, her emotions once again cast aside for the more important word of men.

Draupadi thought of the everyday battles that ravaged her innocent soul. The benediction she felt all this while, she now understood that came from lives past, threatened to rip her being apart with its intensity. She realized that now, perhaps maybe a little too late she thought sadly. For the queen for the longest time, conceived her boon of five husbands a curse because what else can it be to bathe in the intense brightness of men, the likes of which this earth had never seen before! The five Pandavas, each one the son of a Deva, were born on earth to establish righteousness, to kill adharma, and purge Earth of her heavy weight.

The five Pandavas, her husbands, flickered with the radiance of many worlds, the splendour of a million stars who scorched Draupadi many times, repeatedly. They cared for her deeply but despite all their affection, they themselves recklessly battled their own demons. Sahadeva, who relished his wisdom among all living beings and could not stand to be second. Nakul, whose vanity was so immense it stung. Arjuna, the intensely insecure warrior, his every breath only a strive towards perfection and greatness in everything he touched, including his wife. Bheema, with his boastfulness and exceeding battle thirst and Yudhishthira, the eldest Pandava, an insistent gambler, who loved wine too much and desired glory at all costs.

Still yet, she served them, satisfied their unique needs, and made herself indispensable but it was never enough. She went into exile with them when it was not needed, subjected her body to all elements, lived a harsh life, often went to bed hungry, slept on the bare floor because she knew her fate lay alongside theirs. She would live the way they did for they were all one in mind and soul. But, nothing she did earned her their irrefutable loyalty. For, despite their vast power, none of them could show the chutzpah when it mattered to her the most: not at court in Hastinapur when her inebriated husband, the wise and dharma bound Yudhishthira, staked her as a bet and then lost her. Not when Dushashana put his filthy hands on her, dragging her into court by her hair. Not when every single hero present in the court that day saw Draupadi being stripped off her clothes, but no one stopped the sheer injustice being meted out to the queen of Indraprastha. Not when violence against a woman was allowed to be continued in the presence of men who were born to destroy adharma! No one spoke, no one stopped the abuse. It was yet again, another pattern, permitted to permeate in Draupadi's life as if she did not matter, as if she did not even exist!

Draupadi knew what mattered most to the Pandavas was themselves and their honour. An honour that did not include their wife, her cries for help, her maltreatment at the hands of men over and over again throughout her life. Despite his several advances and Draupadi's repeated call for aid, Yudhishthira refused to help her when Keechak tried to force himself on her. There were other, more pressing matters to consider and keep in mind during their year incognito, she was told. Her honour, her consent, threats made to her person were not the most important. It was best she kept to herself and kept things quiet. Now was not the time for justice for a woman, she was told.

It was not important when Jayadratha tried to kidnap and rape her. He was a relative, their cousin's husband, Yudhishthira had said. How could we make our cousin a widow? Such actions were excessive, unwarranted, and gratuitous. Surely, Jayadratha did not deserve to die for such a small crime, her husbands concurred, yet again undermining Draupadi and her honour.

Each incident, each act of assault was met with diabolical explanations instead of the immediate urgency of justice it deserved. The dharma bound Yudhishthira always found a way to not act, to not dish out justice for his wife. Draupadi often wondered what kind of king he would be who always found a way to explain his way out of things instead of taking swift action to benefit those who had been ill-treated.

What happened to her, the insults cast on her, the assaults flung on her, the untoward name calling, irresponsible blaming for being the cause of the Great War were never treated with the horror they justified. Her concerns dismissed, her cry for fairness ignored. Here was Draupadi, no ordinary woman, being treated like a mere commoner. For how can the woman married to the five greatest warriors of all time be ordinary?

No one cared enough to understand her struggles. The divinity left within her unwittingly helped her cope with the fire and with her strife. Draupadi knew that now; but it was after a lifetime of trials and efforts that had left her exhausted, dazed with the inadvertent belief that she was naught. Her toils were for naught. Her existence was for naught. Her womanhood, outside her gender's anatomy, was for naught.

Despite extraordinarily little support, Draupadi fought alone, tirelessly waging the war her heroic warrior husbands did not have the courage for. She did it all by herself, her only genuine companion guiding her, unknowingly, unaware of her true being, continuing to fight upstream for what mattered to her the most—the fair treatment of a woman.

This queen, the greatest of all times, battled both internal and external demons every day, never received love the way she most desired, lost all her children, suffered vehement losses, endured many physical and verbal assaults but stood valiantly, despite it all fighting for her rightful place in her story and the story of the land she belonged to.

Until now, she thought none of it mattered, none of it was substantive and none of it had the power to change anything. Until this moment.

Because, here was Draupadi, the Adi Shakti, the primordial energy of the universe without beginning or end, present in everything, the spark who lit it all in motion. Here was the redeemer of the universe, the power of creation, the creative yogic shakti, the divine life and joy, the power of transformation, the mother who was nature herself who existed forever and through time. Here was Draupadi, her divine cosmic self, truly embracing her being with the realization that nothing flowed without her for she mattered more, above everyone else. Here was the understanding that her mortal self was but a shell of the deep divinity Draupadi harboured within her, across time, across lives.

For the first time in a while, Draupadi smiled.

"Mahadev, I owe you an apology," the queen began.

"An apology for what, Maharani?" Mahadev asked surprised.

"When you came to me at Somnath and offered me the chance to go with you, I will admit, I was very sceptical on what it would entail and how it would help."

"I know," Mahadev said. "You told me so."

Draupadi smirked. "Perhaps, but not in so many words. I, however, felt it. I was not sure about what you were suggesting and whether it would change anything. But, I was so desperate, I was willing to try it."

"You had faith," Mahadev corrected her.

Draupadi nodded in acknowledgement. "Yes, faith in you."

"And, did I let you down?"

"No, Mahadev. You have opened my eyes to the immeasurable nature of this universe. For that, I owe you immensely."

"You do not owe me anything, Maharani. You may not know, but I have my own stake in this."

"What do you stand to gain, Mahadev?" Draupadi asked puzzled.

Mahadev smiled. "Everything," he said, his voice barely a whisper.

"Are you ready to move on, O queen?" Mahadev questioned.

"Yes, but where are we going now?" Draupadi asked.

"To the Nishadha kingdom. Tell me, Yajnaseni, do you know about the great queens of the Nishadha kingdom?"

"I have heard of Nala's wife Damayanti, my Lord."

"Ah yes, Damayanti was a queen but she was not a ruler. Do you know of the ruler queens of the Nishadhas?"

"I do not, Mahadev."

"The Nishadhas are one of the oldest people of the land. For eons, they have protected and conserved the earth. Their deep respect for the environment, the way they have shown deference to the land by taking only what they need and giving back whenever they can, is admirable. Over time, as humans cease to show reverence for Earth and plunder her instead, the Nishadhas will serve to be an example everyone can live by."

"What is the chief occupation of the Nishadhas, Mahadev?"

"Mainly hunting and fishing. Since they live in the area where the mighty Ganga flows, many of them also help travellers cross the river. You may remember King Guha from Treta yuga when he helped Rama, Sita, and Lakshmana cross the river after they left Kosala?"

"I do," Draupadi nodded. "I also remember seeing a massive tank complex but was not sure of its purpose."

"Yes," Mahadev replied. "As I said earlier, the Nishadhas learned how to strategically use the land for their advantage while causing minimal harm. The tank complex was a means to avoid floods in the land during monsoon and served as a primary source of water supply. Whatever was not used was returned to the Ganga towards the east. This system was the most ingenious and resourceful way of conserving water in its time. Many others emulated it for its sheer efficiency and zero waste."

"Who designed it, Mahadev?"

"The ruler of Nishadha, Queen Dhruv."

"Dhruv, the name sounds very familiar," Draupadi said, searching her memory for where she had heard it before. "Also, is that not a man's name?"

"Dhruv was the daughter of King Uttanapada of Nishadha. The Nishadhas did not believe in gender differentiation. Of course, they understood there was the male, the female, and the all-composite gender but they did not believe in following specific rules around gender."

"What is the all-composite gender, Mahadev?" Draupadi asked.

Mahadev smiled. "The all-composite gender is the union of the male and the female, but neither on its own, complete in itself, the root and womb of all creation."

"That sounds like your Ardhanarishvara form, my Lord."

"It *is* the Ardhanarishvara form but in humans, Maharani. Biologically, it is impossible to create a human that is half man and half woman, hence the form shows up differently in mortals."

"How so, Mahadev?"

"In humans, the Ardhanarishvara shows up as a composite of the body and the soul; meaning the body may belong to a gender, while the soul belongs to the opposite gender and vice versa."

"So, that would mean a man in body form maybe a woman in soul form or the other way around?"

"Yes, it could work that way. A male could have certain female elements, or a female could possess male aspects. Remember, Maharani, every human form is a manifestation of divinity. Ardhanarishvara is the perfect synthesis of male and female form, a reminder that Prakriti and Purusha are intertwined, the masculine and feminine energies are inseparable; that one cannot function without the other. Although they are castrated and often ridiculed, those who embody the all-composite gender are sacred, serving as a consistent reminder of my all-pervading nature."

"I understand, Mahadev. I must admit I have never really given the all-composite gender much thought. But now, I realize their importance and true meaning."

"The true test of being human is whether you can evolve in your thinking and learn to do better. I would say, Maharani, you are doing well on both those fronts."

Draupadi grinned upon hearing rare praise from the Lord.

"So, back to the Nishadhas," Mahadev continued, "Queen Dhruv was an extraordinarily successful female ruler. She was a trained military leader who also knew how to use technology to advance her kingdom and promote prosperity among her subjects. The canal is but one example of her ingenuity. She invented many such improvements that ranked the Nishadhas among pioneers.

Queen Dhruv was also a devotee of Lord Vishnu. As a child, she undertook severe penance, giving up food and drink, and only focussing her being around the worship of Vishnu. Over time, her penance became so intense that her breathing stopped causing all three worlds to stop breathing too. That is when the gods requested Lord Vishnu to appear before Dhruv and grant her a wish."

"What wish did she ask for, Mahadev?"

"She wanted to be united with the Supreme Being, but Lord Vishnu stopped short of granting her that. He asked her to go back and rule her kingdom, as was her duty, and promised her salvation when she eventually died."

"Why did she engage in such hard penance as a child, Lord?"

"Growing up she heard many tales of Lord Vishnu that fostered her immense devotion. After Sage Narada visited her and described the Lord further, all she wanted was to be united with him."

"So much intensity in such young a child," Draupadi observed, admiringly.

"Yes, she burnt bright, and she burnt long. Upon her death, her eldest daughter came to the throne and continued her mother's long, just, and prosperous rule. The kingdom of Nishadha was in incredibly good hands until it came time for King Vena."

"Was he not a good ruler, Mahadev?"

"He started off as a very wise ruler, but over time became extremely evil and corrupt."

"The power went to his head, like Ravana."

"Yes, it did. But, unlike Ravana, Vena was no scholar or Maha-Brahman. His rule meant decline in the conditions for all living beings, ruthless plunder of the environment and wasting the natural resources of the land. Vena went against everything the good people of the Nishadhas believed in and had been practicing since the beginning of time. Things got so bad at one point that Earth refused to provide crops to humans anymore. Mother Earth took the form of a cow and went into hiding. There were severe food shortages everywhere and many natural disasters that led to considerable loss of life. Unable to bear it any further, the people of Nishadha started to rebel."

"Oh my!" gasped Draupadi. "It sounds like the end of days, Mahadev."

"Had the seers not intervened, it would definitely have been the end of days for the Nishadha kingdom. Their timely act saved the people."

"What did the seers do, my Lord?"

"They murdered King Vena."

"What! Murdered him?" Draupadi exclaimed. "Was it that bad?"

"It was, as you said earlier, like the end of days. The king had to be removed to save the people. The seers gave Vena a choice to abdicate but when he refused, they killed him."

"Sounds gruesome."

"Yes, but necessary. Sometimes it is important to take one life to save countless more."

"Yes, it is, but what happens when countless lives are lost on both sides?" the queen asked pensively reflecting on the battle at Kurukshetra.

"That is called war, Maharani. So, after the seers killed Vena, they prayed to Lord Vishnu for a king. A new ruler who would occupy King Vena's body but not his spirit. For the good of all, Lord Vishnu consented. He rubbed Vena's left arm and the good king Pritha was born."

"Did King Pritha belong to the all-composite gender?" Draupadi asked.

"He did. Lord Vishnu created the king from his left arm. It was no wonder he identified with the all-composite gender."

"Because the left side of the body is feminine, and the right side is masculine?" Draupadi asked, pre-emptively.

Mahadev nodded his assent. "Yes. Regardless of gender, each human contains feminine and masculine energies. Contrary to the all-composite, when the gender of the body matches that of the soul, humans identify themselves as male or female. This does not mean though that they do not have the energies of the opposite gender for as you correctly pointed out, the left side harbours female energies, whereas the right side holds the masculine energies.

King Pritha was male in body but female in mind and soul. He was a great king who knew his birth was brought forth to calm the chaos and bring peace back to the kingdom. His first task was to pacify Earth so she would agree to grow crops again. For that, he first had to find her."

"Mother Earth, who was hiding somewhere in the guise of a cow," Draupadi said.

"Indeed. To find her, King Pritha had to undertake severe penance. Finally, pleased with the king's penance, Mother Earth decided to appear and seeing the change in Vena, now Pritha, agreed to forgive past mistakes. Pritha promised to treat Mother Earth with gratitude and respect and worked the land diligently. Pleased with the king's work, Earth returned all the crops and the land started to thrive again. There was an abundance of resources everywhere and life for the Nishadhas flourished once more."

"Is this why Earth is also called Prithvi? Because of King Pritha?"

"You are very perceptive, Maharani. King Pritha brought Earth back to her pleasant state. Yes, that is why she chose to name herself Prithvi, after the good King Pritha.

The kingdom of Nishadha continued their prosperous rule for many centuries after. During the time of Lord Rama, King Guha ruled the land. He was a wise king who understood the importance of Earth and gave her the respect she deserves. Respect that unfortunately will wane with time," Mahadev said.

"You mean during the latter part of Kali yuga?" Draupadi asked, her skin shuddering at her earlier visions.

"Yes. A time during which humans will exploit technology to such an extent it will cause irreversible harm to the Earth, when natural disasters will occur frequently and with increased intensity. When the water, air, and land will be so polluted, it will cause massive loss of life, loss of habitats, and complete extinction of many species. But, perhaps the most important effect of human activity will be the loss of ice sheets that cover the

Earth, significantly increasing water levels and causing many great floods."

Draupadi shivered with fear. "Is there any recourse for humanity, my Lord?" she asked.

"It is pre-ordained, Maharani. Humans must complete the cycle, Kali yuga is when the cycle of *pralaya* enters its final stages. Things need to get to a point where they are bad enough to cause the Great Dissolution so everything can begin anew. Humans can prolong the inevitable if their greed allows them to, but they cannot stop what is already foretold."

King Nala sat in his receiving chamber eagerly awaiting Sage Damana's arrival. The rishi had some urgent business with him, the king was told. Nala was very keen to find out how he may help the great sage.

"O great King Nala, glory be to you and your kingdom," the rishi blessed the king.

"O Sage Damana, honoured is the Nishadha kingdom for you have entered it. Tell me, how can I help you?" the king, providing a seat to the rishi, asked.

"The time has come for you to pick a queen," the sage began. "A king as virtuous as you, needs a queen equally so. I know just the woman who will complete your life and wash away your unhappiness."

"It is true I am unhappy; O Sage, for I have not been able to find this kingdom a queen and me a suitable wife. I have travelled far and wide in search of the woman who will complete me but my heart refuses to accept anyone."

"I know who your heart desires and who it shall accept with glee and complete favour."

"Tell me of this great lady, O Sage. Who is she and where can I find her?"

"Her name is Damayanti, and she is the princess of Vidarbha where the pious King Bhimadev rules. The princess is now of marriageable age and her father has arranged a swayamvara for her. Princess Damayanti is a devout woman, well versed in the Vedas. Her beauty is legendary among all the *lokas* (planes). Not only is she morally your equal but is also a kind, charitable woman who believes in the good of all. She will prove a consummate partner for you and a worthy queen for Nishadha. Go attend her swayamvara and win the heart of this devotee of Goddess Parvati. She is the mother your future children need," Rishis Damana advised King Nala.

King Nala, hopeful, bowed to the rishi for his guidance and made his way to the Vidarhba kingdom to participate in Princess Damayanti's swayamvara.

King Nala could not think of anything else. Every minute, every day of his waking life was spent in thoughts of Damayanti. He had hopelessly fallen in love with a woman he had never seen before, only having heard countless praises of her mind, body, and soul. In Vidharba, among the many kings who were in attendance for Damayanti's swayamvara, King Nala wandered the royal gardens lovesick for the princess.

Walking past the wide expanse of medicinal plants heavily used to cure various ailments, King Nala came upon a vast array of trees bearing large clusters of crinkly purple and white petals of Jarul. The land glowed with the intensity of the smell, a sweet, buoyed fragrance that spread for several miles. Birds chirped happily in the summer sun, content with the natural forces that bound everything around them.

King Nala imagined himself walking hand in hand with the princess, enjoying the sight that lay around them. He could almost touch Damayanti; in his dreams she was so real he knew she longed for him as much as he did for her. King Nala did not know what he would do if Damayanti would not become his wife. Nothing else held any meaning for the king anymore. He needed Damayanti as he needed air to survive. His life was incomplete without her presence.

Wandering through the gardens, lost in his forlorn thoughts, the King saw a golden-winged swan land on the grass. Nala ran forward and immediately caught the swan by its neck. Adoring the beauty in his hands, he decided to present the swan to the princess as a token of his sincerity and deep love.

"Nala, let me go," the swan said.

"You speak in a human tongue?" asked the shocked king.

"Not only do I speak the human tongue, I know what aches your heart so. If you release me, I promise to go to Princess Damayanti and sing your praises before the swayamvara tomorrow. I know your heart pines for her. I will tell her there is no better match for her."

Nala blushed at the sound of the princess's name. "You promise?"

"I do," the swan responded.

"I will release you. Please tell the princess I am desperately in love with her, and my life will not be fulfilled until the day she is mine," Nala said and released the golden bird.

The swan, true to its word, arrived at the royal chambers of Princess Damayanti. The princess sat on her bed, a book in her hand, her mind elsewhere. She looked like she was in love, the swan noticed. A look he had just seen in King Nala.

The swan called out to the princess. "O dear princess, pray tell me what thoughts distract you so?"

Her thoughts interrupted; the princess looked at the window towards the swan. "Who are you and what do you want from me, swan?" she asked.

"I have come here to tell you about the virtuous King Nala."

Damayanti's rosy cheeks turned red at the mention of the king's name. "I see," the swan continued. "You pine for him as he does for you."

"He pines for me?" the princess threw the book to the ground and ran to the swan. "Tell me everything, swan. Tell me what you know of the great King Nala," Damayanti said, the words rushing out of her mouth.

The swan told Damayanti everything. That night Damayanti did not sleep. She could not wait for morning. The day she would finally become Nala's wife.

The next day, kings dressed in their best clothes and fanciest jewels made their way to the swayamvara. The four gods, Indra, Varun, Agni, and Yama, came too. They saw King Nala who was also on his way, grateful that the day had finally arrived. The Gods were impressed with the morality and quiet dignity of this man. Feeling jealous, the Gods chalked a plan to remove Nala from possible contention at the swayamvara.

Approaching him, Lord Indra said, "You are King Nala, are you not? I am Indra and need a favour. Would you help carry a message?"

The king, surprised at Indra's presence, bowed to the God. "I will do anything you ask, my Lord."

"We are headed to the swayamvara of Princess Damayanti. Go and tell her we are on our way and she should choose one of us as her husband."

Nala's heart sank. "But, my Lord, I am headed in the same direction and wish to marry the princess. Pray excuse me from this task."

"You promised you would do anything. Are you going back on your word?" Indra hissed at Nala.

Realizing his dilemma, Nala agreed to carry the message to Damayanti. "But, her rooms will be well guarded, my Lord. How will I get in?" he asked.

"Leave that to me. I will arrange it so that you can enter without being seen," Indra responded, haughtily.

Heartbroken, Nala made his way to Damayanti's chambers. Stunning in her bridal clothes, Damayanti sat amidst her friends, the glow on her face rivalling the shine of the full moon. Bedecked in heavy jewellery and fragrant flowers, the princess looked like an apsara, her youth and virtue shining through her. Nala looked at her despondently. This woman would not become his wife after all, he thought sadly.

Startled by his presence, the princess got up. "Who are you and how did you manage to enter in here?" Damayanti asked.

Nala bowed to the princess. "O beautiful one, my name is Nala and I come to you as a messenger of the Gods. They are on their way to your swayamvara and wish that you choose one of them as your husband."

"You are Nala?" the princess exclaimed. "But, I thought you were also participating in my swayamvara. Why are you here speaking on behalf of the Gods?" she asked, her heart thundering in the presence of the man she so desperately wished to wed.

"I gave the Gods my word before knowing what they wished for. They wish to marry you," Nala replied, sadly. "I wish to marry you with all my heart, but I now know that day will never come."

"But, I wish to marry you too, Nala. My heart aches for your love and I have already chosen you as my husband."

Nala's heart rose with hope. Could it still happen that he would marry this glorious woman standing before him?

"I am but a mortal, O princess. The Gods may get terribly upset if you do not choose one of them," Nala said.

The princess thought for a moment. "I thank you, Nala, for coming here today. The matter of choice lies in my hands and I shall make the decision I want. Please tell the Gods in the presence of everybody, I shall choose you as my husband."

Nala left the royal chambers, his heart soaring with happiness.

At the appointed hour, Damayanti entered the swayamvara hall where an unusual sight greeted her. Seated among the guests who hoped to win her hand, were five Nalas. Puzzled, Damayanti concluded the Gods were playing a trick on her. Her hands bowed, she spoke, "O Gods, with faith in my heart, I have chosen Nala to be my husband. I urge you to please reveal him to me. For my yearning and morality cannot marry anyone else;

it will not be love but a farce. I pray to you to please let me marry Nala."

The four assembled Gods realized the true power of Damayanti's devotion, a love far stronger than anything they had shown. They knew they could not withstand the power of a woman's righteousness; especially that of an ardent worshipper of Goddess Parvati, the *Adi Parashakti* (primordial force). Realizing their mistake, the four Gods assumed their true form and conferred special blessings upon Damayanti and Nala. They would always be there for the couple; the Gods assured the duo.

In the presence of all the guests, Damayanti then placed her garland around Nala's neck. Nala and Damayanti were proclaimed husband and wife.

"Nala and Damayanti returned to the kingdom, happy and joyous. They were extremely wise rulers who leaned on each other for guidance and help. Sage Damana was prescient in his words about Damayanti. She was exactly the queen the kingdom and the king needed," Mahadev told Draupadi.

"I am glad to see this tender love story between Nala and Damayanti. So glad to see they both got what their heart ached for. It fills me with joy to see them so happy."

"Yes, it is a warm, loving feeling, no doubt. But, your emotions are high not just because of the strength of their bond but also because of the strength of your bond with them. They were your parents. It is only understandable you feel so strongly about their union."

"I must admit, Mahadev. It is a strange feeling to go back and see what happened with my parents in all these lives," Draupadi smiled.

"I take your word, Maharani," Mahadev said laughing.

"I do not see any children so far though, Mahadev. When am I born?" Draupadi asked.

"Unfortunately, many years passed before Nala and Damayanti were able to conceive a child. After many unsuccessful years, the royal couple initiated the Putrakameshti yagna when Agni Deva came back to visit them. Sad to see Nala and Damayanti so forlorn, the God of Fire gave Damayanti a special drink which would help her conceive. Soon after, Damayanti was pregnant and gave birth to twins, a boy, Indrasena and a girl, Indrasenaa, later known as Nalayani."

Draupadi nodded and smiled at yet another connection to Lord Agni. She was beginning to understand the reason for her own, internal fire.

"Damayanti was an ardent devotee of Goddess Parvati. Did Lord Agni bless her with the *ansh* (aspect) of Parvati within him?"

Mahadev smiled approvingly. "Yes, Damayanti was blessed with the *ansh* of the Goddess."

"It is all making sense," Draupadi remarked. "This knowledge is so liberating to the soul. I wish I would have had it earlier but realize that there is a time and place for everything."

"You are right, O queen. Your time has finally come."

"Do you know the story of how Nala lost his kingdom?" Mahadev asked.

"I do," Draupadi said, her eyes wide, her head nodding in dislike. "Nala, like Yudhishthira, liked to gamble too much and lost his kingdom in a bet to his cousin."

"Yes, against Damayanti's sound advice, Nala chose to play with Pushkara, his cousin, who had always been envious of the king. When he started losing steadily in the game, Damayanti and the courtiers urged Nala to stop, but he did not."

"Inebriated men, playing a game of dice, rarely take the advice of women. I have personal experience with such ghastly situations," Draupadi said, her voice resentful.

"Unfortunately, you do, and I am sorry you had to experience that level of assault. It is never excusable or forgiven."

Draupadi looked at Mahadev tenderly. Until this moment, he had never uttered anything condemning a human experience. His words made her look at him in a different light. Mahadev smiled at her sadly. Their gaze met, a moment of lighting passing through the queen. Draupadi reflexively looked away. She felt somewhat nervous, like her control was slipping away.

"When Damayanti saw what was happening, she immediately sent her twins away to her father in Vidarbha," Mahadev continued. "She had a foreboding of how this would end. And, in the end, Damayanti was right. Nala lost his kingdom to his greedy cousin and walked away from his old life into exile. Damayanti followed him."

Draupadi shook her head in quiet disbelief. The same story again. At least, Damayanti was not staked. She quietly thanked Nala for showing that level of deference towards his wife. One that was not afforded to her by Yudhishthira.

"It is amazing how the pattern of what happened to Nala and Damayanti is so similar to the Pandavas and my life," Draupadi said.

"Losing everything at the game of dice and going into exile, yes," Mahadev said. "But, that is where the similarity ends. The Pandavas never abandoned you or left you alone in a forest. No matter how bad the circumstances were, you always had your husbands' support. Maybe, they did not always do what you wanted them to but eventually they avenged every insult, every assault, and every person who wronged you. You may not know or believe this, Maharani, but for the Pandavas, you, Draupadi are and always will be the most important person. Their devotion towards you is unquestionable and infinite."

Draupadi reflected on Mahadev's words. He was right, she admitted much to her chagrin. No matter what, her husbands never left her side, firmly rooted next to her. Maybe, they were not so bad after all, she thought amusingly.

"I am a lucky woman, Mahadev. I may sound acrimonious and harsh sometimes, but I am blessed for I have the undying love of five great men. And, truth be told, I love them too with all my heart. I know people wonder how a woman can find love for five men at one time in her heart. I know they accuse me of being partial towards one husband and caring less for another, but I love them all equally. My heart beats the same way when I am in Sahadeva's arms or when I am sharing moments with Bheema."

"So, it is not true? You do not love Arjuna the most? You only allowed him to bring another wife into the palace. Some may say that is proof that he holds a special place in your heart," the Lord teased Draupadi.

"Arjuna won my swayamvara effortlessly. It is true my heart craved another but Arjuna's devotion and love eventually won me over. As far as Subhadra is concerned, she managed to make her way into the palace thanks to the mischief of Krishna. Over time, though, I started to love her as a sister, and we became very good friends. I did not have any friends in Panchala, Mahadev. Life has been strange for me, not because of the hardship, but because I had no idea how to do basic things like make friends, love a sister, be a mother. Nothing about my life has been typical, right from my birth to marriage to five men to even being here with you today," Draupadi said.

"I can only imagine, Maharani. It sure has been an extraordinary experience for you, one you have met with astounding resilience. I do not fathom to know the depths of your heart, Maharani, but I am curious about one thing. May I ask?" the Lord besought.

"You can ask me anything, Mahadev," the queen replied.

"Who did you wish to marry, if not Arjuna?"

"Karna," Draupadi said without hesitation.

"Ah yes, Karna," Mahadev said, softly. "What a mighty warrior and a brave soul he was. Another misunderstood human."

"Yes, he was. I misunderstood him too. He did not deserve that level of hatred from me. He was a good man who did some terrible things. But, he knew he was not on the side of dharma and that his cause would lose."

"He did, indeed. But, he pushed on anyway for that was the experience his soul needed in this life," Mahadev explained.

"Sad but I cannot judge his life nor his actions," Draupadi said resigned. "The man had so much potential. He could have been king of Hastinapur instead of Yudhishthira for he was the eldest Pandava. The Pandavas would have given him everything he had ever wanted—respect, trust, adoration, legitimacy, even loyalty. Instead, he chose to fight for his friend."

"The friend who gave him so much and stood by him when no one else did," Mahadev added.

"Yes, Duryodhana gave Karna friendship and support when he needed the most. I understand why Karna felt indebted to him. I feel the same way towards Shri Krishna, who came to me in my direst hours. I would do anything for him," Draupadi said, her voice full of love.

"And, he for you," Mahadev said, quietly.

Unable to bear the state of his wife and how he had contributed to it, Nala left Damayanti alone in the forest. Eventually, he made his way towards King Rituparna, the ruler of Ayodhya, where he worked as the palace cook and tended the king's horses in the stable. Damayanti, despondent on losing her husband, arrived in the kingdom of Chedi, and worked as a maid to the queen and the princess. The King of Vidarbha, worried about his daughter and her husband, sent men in search of them who finally came to Chedi and found Damayanti.

Damayanti reunited with her parents and twins; thereafter, all attention turned towards finding Nala. The king whose appearance had changed after a snake bite, continued to stay away from his wife and family, thinking himself unworthy. Damayanti's quick thinking and persistence ultimately identified Nala, who then learned the game of dice from King Rituparna, returned to challenge Pushkara and won back his kingdom. The happy couple, at long last, returned to Nishadha, having crossed many obstacles, and learnt a valuable lesson about life. Their children by their side, Nala and Damayanti ruled over a prosperous time for the kingdom. After Nala's death, his son Indrasena took over and followed in his father's footsteps. Daughter Indrasenaa, who had an extraordinarily strong bond with her father, changed her name to Nalayani and married the King of Panchal, Mudgala.

"This is where your final story before assuming the life of Draupadi begins, O great one. I hope this journey although very painful at times has caused you revelations and helped you understand your true form," Mahadev said to Draupadi.

"It has," she said. The transformation within her was overwhelming but she did not yet have all the words to process and identify it.

I also see how I, as Nalayani, was an ancestor to Drupada, my father and the last king of Panchala," Draupadi said.

"Yes, eleven generations after the rule of King Mudgala, your father Drupada took the throne of Panchala. A kingdom now ruled by your husband, Yudhishthira."

King Mudgala and Queen Nalayani's wedding was celebrated with great pomp and glory. Nalayani, petite and delicate featured, intelligent in expression but quiet in demeanour, with her dark skin tone and olive brown eyes that shone with excitement, stood next to her new husband, her mind whirling with anticipation. King Mudgala, medium built with a large head, was dressed in a long tunic with exquisite brocade, golden gloves over his hands, apathy on his face. The kingdom rejoiced, celebrating the union of the royal couple.

King Mudgala, though, was not interested in the celebrations or in his wedding. Seeing his wife as only a means to an end, to further his kingdom, the king approached his bride on their wedding night, where a restive Nalayani awaited him.

"Nalayani," the king addressed his wife, "although I am king of Panchala and reign over this land, my true devotion lies elsewhere."

Nalayani's heart sank. These were not the words a bride expected to hear on her wedding night. Her heart, filled with fear, started beating loudly.

"My life is completely devoted to Lord Vishnu and I only wish to work on that which attains me unification with the Supreme Being."

Nalayani took a deep breath inwardly. At least, it was not another woman.

"I know I am expected to produce an heir for this kingdom. I will do that, but I would like to warn you to not expect me to perform any other marital duties or other duties befitting a husband. I shall not be able to fulfil those for my mind only works in the service of the great Lord."

Nalayani's heart sank. She did not understand any of this. All she wanted was a happy marriage, a husband who would care for her, look after her, and protect her like her father loved her mother. This man standing before her was speaking words she could not comprehend. How can a husband not love his wife? How can a married man wish to abandon his responsibilities and go elsewhere? How was this fair? A thousand thoughts ran through Nalayani's mind, but she held them back. It was not her nature to speak. Life had handed her a cruel verdict, but still she withheld her thoughts.

The king then lay next to his new queen and consummated their marriage. The following morning, King Mudgala left the royal chambers before his queen had even opened her eyes.

"What is with the kings of Panchala? I will admit my experience is only limited to my father, Drupada, but now I see Mudgala and I cannot help but ask. Their actions can only be described as abusive towards their daughters or their wives. Why is it so, Mahadev?"

"Sage Mudgala was an extremely complicated soul. He was highly learned and in his own ways loved his wife, although his calling lay elsewhere."

"How can one call this behaviour love, Mahadev? The man is using Nalayani to secure his kingdom and continue his dynasty. He told her as much," Draupadi objected.

"Yes, he did and over time the couple had four children: Maudgalya, Vadhryasva, Divodas, and Ahalya. I agree Mudgala did not believe in having a relationship with his wife but she, nevertheless, served him truthfully, with all the love and devotion. When his health started to deteriorate, her attention to him became even more pronounced. He was never a handsome king, but the disease affected his appearance, and he became very unsightly. Nalayani still never left his side, continuing her ardent service of her husband."

Draupadi shook her head in incredulity. "So unfortunate. Is that why the king was wearing golden gloves at his wedding?"

"Yes, to hide his sickness. Nalayani, for her part, had accepted the reality of her life. Her mission now lay in making sure her sick husband was well taken care of and that his worship of Lord Vishnu would continue unabated. Mudgala renounced his kingdom, handing everything to his son Vadhryasva. Nalayani, accompanied her husband, set up their ashram and made sure she could continue to take care of him. Her husband's mission became her mission. That is the kind of person Nalayani was. An honourable soul."

"She had to take care of her husband like he is some child," Draupadi interjected, her tone bitter.

Mahadev smiled. "I do not condone Mudgala's actions either but remember the nature of humanity, Maharani. Mudgala's life simply lay elsewhere. It was an ill-fated match for Nalayani but things tend to come full circle, eventually."

"Yes, they do but that does not mean injustice does not make one angry."

"No, it does not at all," Mahadev reaffirmed.

"What happened at the ashram then? Did Mudgala make her work morning, noon, and night?"

"He did. As his sickness progressed, Mudgala got progressively cantankerous and unpredictable. He would get angry with her for no reason at all. While he sought the divine with his severe meditation, the rishi increasingly placed unreasonable expectations on his wife. He would send her up mountains, and down caverns, on the ledges of cliffs, to fetch medicinal herbs or some other plant of importance to him. He would let her eat only after he had eaten, make her wash him several times a day, and many such bizarre demands.

He also made her sell her last piece of jewellery as payment, one given to her by her father on her wedding day so he could have sex with another woman. For this, Mudgala made Nalayani carry him in a basket to the woman's home, much to the amusement and taunts of everyone in the market. He also made Nalayani carry him back when he was done," Mahadev said, trying hard not to judge, his voice failing him utterly.

"Poor Nalayani. This man is beastly. I wonder why she put up with him and his ridiculous antics. No one deserves such an assault on their morality, especially someone as noble as Nalayani," Draupadi lamented. "Mudgala was trying to break her," she said, conclusively, "but he did not succeed."

"Yes, he was. Although he believed in simple living, high thinking, and had the highest level of patience amongst all the rishis, somehow all of that dissipated when he saw his wife. One day though, things changed."

The rishi sat on the ground, waiting for Nalayani to serve him his meal. He looked at his wife, this immeasurable woman who had served him without any expectations, never asking for anything in return, dutiful in all her tasks. He had put her through the toughest of tests and she had passed.

Nalayani turned towards her husband placing a plate of rice, roti, and potatoes with beans cooked in a sauce he liked, in front of him. She looked at the sage, beckoning him to eat, a tender smile upon her lips to see her husband content. Their eyes met. Nalayani was confused. "What did the sage want?" she thought. She waited for his next command, his next unseemly request which Nalayani would laugh at but invariably fulfil for how could she deny the man she had married? With the name of Lord Shiva on her lips, her mind engrossed in His glory, Nalayani would always give her husband whatever he asked for; no matter how unseeming or impossible.

"Nalayani," the sage spoke, affectionately. Her heart froze for she had never heard him show such warmth towards her. Nalayani looked up at him, her heart beating, her mind befuddled.

"You are the purest of all in this world, the most devoted wife any man can ever find upon this Earth. Know that I am neither sick nor diseased. I had assumed this form and continued this charade to test you," the rishi said.

Nalayani was speechless. Part of her was relieved, the other fuming. She reminded herself of her devotion to her husband, to Lord Shiva, whose marriage she had hoped to emulate in her life. Her eyes wide, she continued to look upon her husband, the sage Mudgala.

"You are the most self-possessed and untiring woman a man could have as wife. Ask me for any boon and I shall fulfil it," the sage told his wife.

"Any boon?" she thought. Nalayani's mind spun with the possibilities. Too much was taking place too quickly. Her husband looking at her with love, telling her he was not sick, and now she could ask for any boon? Her life was changing faster than she could keep pace with it. Nalayani sat there, dumbfounded, unable to utter a single word at her husband who stared at her with a bemused curiosity.

"I know I have said this before, but Sage Mudgala's actions are too harsh and not befitting a man of his station. The way I see it, he is simply playing with his innocent wife's emotions," the queen reiterated her objections, disgust in her voice.

Mahadev simply nodded. He concurred with her. The queen's opinion was well founded, as was her rage.

Sage Mudgala asked again. "Speak, O humble wife. What would you like?"

"What would I like? Husband, I do not know what to say. For you speaking to me in this form is the biggest gift I could ever ask for," Nalayani said, her mind still a whirlwind at events.

"There must be something your heart desires. Maybe a new sari? Or perhaps a lavish life away from these austerities? Tell me. What would you want most from your husband?"

Nalayani did not know for she had never given any importance to her needs or desires. What would she want from her husband? Her mind, however, kept repeating Mudgala's last word. Husband. Husband. Husband. Husband. Husband.

Instantly, Nalayani knew the answer.

"If you say you are not sickly or diseased, discard this form and become your true self. I would like to experience marital bliss with you. Let us leave this ashram and travel the worlds, both known and unknown, experiencing each other. I would like to know true love, a happy marriage, and uninhibited passion with you."

The sage acquiesced immediately. Mudgala discarded his old form, his creaking body and unsightly appearance gone in a flash, replaced by a strong man, with a nimble body, his face shining with youth, his person warm and fervent, abounding with desire.

Nalayani flung herself into the rishi's arms, their embrace aroused and eager. Arm in arm, the two lovers travelled across the worlds, in each other's company ravishing themselves passionately for many years. Mudgala took her to the snow topped mountains of the Himalayas, and down to the deep bottoms of the Sarasvati river, the tropical rain forest of Thar and the white salt desert of Kutch. Nalayani danced gleefully, seeing sights she never imagined to be true. She twirled in the monsoon rain, glaciated in the winter snow, ran at the incoming ocean waves, and slept under the midnight stars, her effervescent being rejoicing in the experience, drinking deeply from her husband's love who did everything to mend his injustice of her past trials.

After many years, Sage Mudgala grew tired of the travels and their ceaseless lovemaking. Longing for his old life, the sage wished to return to the ashram. He turned to his wife. "Nalayani, I grow tired of this life now. Let us go back to the ashram, resume our simple living and our long meditations. How I miss those," he said with yearning. "Will you accompany me back?" he asked her.

Nalayani, whose life was just beginning to blossom, found her husband's words undesirable. She became inimical of Mudgala's longing for his old life, annoyed that he preferred a mundane existence at the ashram instead of spending time with her and the joys that they shared together. She did not share her husband's deep love for an abstinent lifestyle and had no desire to return to it. Summoning her courage, she spoke, "O dear husband, I do not long for the ashram or for the long meditations. This life, with you by my side, exploring this world is so dear to me. Can we not stay a while longer and pleasure each other?" she asked, sincerely.

Mudgala, whose bad temper was returning and turning him to his crotchety form again, exploded at his wife. "How dare you stop me, you harridan? I have spent too many years already satisfying your sexual desires and you still want more? Where does your greed end or is it simply boundless? Your vixen charms cannot trap me in this *Maya* (illusion) any longer. I am a spiritual man and will return to my life, whether you come with me or not."

Sage Mudgala walked away from Nalayani, leaving her heart broken once more. Perhaps, this life was just a mistake, she told herself. Nalayani sobbed, her wailing thundering across the forest, lighting a sudden ray of hope within her. Sitting cross legged, tying her long hair in a bun across the nape of her neck, her golden sari draped across her, closing her eyes, Nalayani invoked the one name that was always present on her lips.

"Shiv. Shiv. Shiv. Shiv," Nalayani repeated the Maha Mrityunjaya mantra, extolling the image of the Lord upon her entire being.

Days passed. The world changed its form across the worlds but was afraid to disturb Nalayani. The power of her devotion rumbled the ground beneath Nalayani's feet so ferociously that Mother Earth appealed to the Lord of all the Worlds to rescue her.

"Visit Nalayani, O Lord of all the Lords. For if not, I may collapse under the intensity of her penance."

The Lord, kind and benevolent, appeared before Nalayani, rousing her from her deep meditation.

"Open your eyes, O Nalayani. I am here," Mahadev announced to the poor woman who had suffered a lifetime of needless travail.

The bewitching person of Lord Shiva graced before Nalayani, a sight that filled her soul and brought tears to her eyes.

"What ails you, O holy woman? Why have you summoned me today? What boon would you like?" Mahadev asked Nalayani.

Tongue tied at the sight before her, Nalayani only murmured, "Husband. Husband. Husband. Husband. Husband."

"You want a husband? What kind of husband would you like, Nalayani?" the Lord asked her.

"Husband," stumbling through her words, Nalayani described her ideal husband to the Lord. "A man who is a paragon of truth, as strong as Hanuman, an ace archer, the most handsome, and most patient of all in this world."

Mahadev's face fell. It would be impossible for such a man to exist. "I cannot do that, Nalayani for such men do not exist anymore. No one man will possess all the qualities you are looking for in a husband. What you ask for is unattainable in one man no matter how valiant he is and how intense your devotion."

Nalayani's heart sank. Even the Gods could not give her what she genuinely wanted. Nevertheless, she persisted. "Nothing is unattainable for you, Mahadev. You are the God of all the Gods. You can make the impossible possible. Please, I pray to you, give me a husband who can satisfy my heart's desire."

"Nalayani, you are asking me to fit the ocean in a pitcher. I cannot do so," Mahadev explained again. He knew Nalayani was standing at the precipice. He tried to pull her back once more.

"There is nothing more I wish for, Pashupatinath," Nalayani said dejected. "If even you cannot give me what I want, what meaning does this world hold for anyone anymore?"

Mahadev sighed. He knew where this would lead. The inexplicable life of Draupadi was taking form and he could not stop it. For he could not refuse this woman before him, even though he tried. Mahadev decided to give Nalayani what she was looking for. She would have to bear the consequences of an intricate boon in an extremely complicated life.

"So be it. May you be blessed with love that embodies all the virtues you are looking for." Mahadev blessed Nalayani and vanished.

Pleased with her success, Nalayani started to invoke Lord Agni. "I have nothing more left in this life, O Lord. Please accept me and rid me of this troublesome existence."

The ruddy figure of the God of Fire appeared and assented to her wish. As she slowly walked into the flames, Nalayani looked upon this world for which she was losing love quickly. Eager to leave it behind, she asked Agni the question burning her inside out, "How many times more do I need to walk through you on this Earth?" she asked, her past lives at once clear as the shining sun in her mind.

"You will walk out of me one last time, Nalayani. When you come back to Earth to end adharma as Draupadi, the wife of the Pandavas and friend of Shri Krishna," he replied.

"Krishna? I wonder who that is," Nalayani mumbled as she entered the fire defeated.

There was nothing left to say. Nothing more to do. Mahadev had shown Draupadi all there was. He hoped it was enough. He hoped he would get what he came for. His wife, in her entirety, back to him. Mahadev waited with bated breath afraid for what was to come next. Even the Lord of All the Worlds was held captive by the love he felt for the woman standing next to him.

The queen was silent. She could feel the vast presence of Mahadev beside her. His persona glowed with a fragrance she had not noticed before. His body shone, the light covering her, bathing her soul with a love she had not known. She felt a pull towards him, a magnetism so strong she felt carried away in its waves. But, Draupadi was not scared. She was no longer worried, concerned, or wary. Her anxiety was washing away, replaced with a clear comprehension of her place in the universe. Her fire that had plagued her for many lifetimes had disappeared, she could no longer feel the intensity of the spirited flames, making her soul felt light, suffused with an ardour, vibrating with an energy of omniscience throughout her.

Draupadi could ask Mahadev why he did what he did, why he blessed her so, but she realized she did not care for the answers anymore. The certainty of it all was clear to her. Draupadi could feel the difference, she understood who she was and why she was. It had all come full circle, perpetuating more than just exhaustive relief, but a beatitude of knowledge, a recall of resolve, intentional in all its forms.

Luminating visions flashed before her eyes.

Her cosmic energy bursting forth pulsating creation. Her manifestation that formed matter, the glue that held totality together, the power of its earliest knowledge, imbibed in every aspect of this universe, marking its beginning, its purpose, and its end.

She in all her forms; Kali, Bhagvati, Bhavani, Ambika, Lalita, Parvati, Kandalini, Java, Durga, and Rajeswari.

She, the mother of time. The impermanence of all things. The source of light that casts away all darkness and doubt. The only truth. All of existence.

She, the boundless space, the limitless void, the lightning force of consciousness, and supreme power. The slayer of ego. The creator of illusion and the destroyer of illusion. The *Nirguna Brahman* universe beyond space and time.

The protective mother of the universe. The primordial Mother Goddess. The origin of all things in *Brahman* (the universe).

She, Durga, impassable, invincible, unassailable, the undefeatable goddess. The subtle feminine force that lights up the world. An embodiment of purity, knowledge, self-realization, and truth.

Her Navadurga forms. Skondamata, Kusumanda, Shailaputri, Kaalratri, Brahmacharini, Maha Gauri, Katyayani, Chandraghanta, and Siddhidatri.

She; *Triyambake*. The three-eyed goddess representing desire, action, and knowledge.

The Sudarshan Chakra spinning around her index finger to destroy evil and promote righteousness.

Her trident, encompassing the three *gunas* (qualities) of the universe—satva, rajas, and tamas.

The demon Raktabija. A dance, the euphoric swirls, the accompanying blood thirst. Mahadev's body underneath her feet, he prostrated to pacify her. His love patient yet all consuming.

Riding a lion. The demon Mahishashura. The beheading. The destruction of tyranny.

Arjuna's invocation to her on the eve of battle. Her divine sanction for their victory. Her tongue spread out on the battlefield, consuming sinners. The slaying of adharma with Vishnu.

Sati. The wedding. The yagna. Daksha. The insults. Agni. Immolation.

King Himavan. Parvati. Her undying resolve. Kama. The third eye. Destruction everywhere. The young yogin who would not give up.

The wedding. His poem to her.

I am the sea and you the wave,
You are Prakriti, and I Purusha.

Nitya. Vedavati. Ravana. Her inextinguishable flame of love for Mahadev. Her failure. Agni.

Chaya. Rama. Panchavati. Ashoka Vatika. Hanuman. Agni.

Nalayani. Mudgala. The hopelessness. Mahadev's boon. Agni.

Agni. Draupadi. Pandavas. She dragged by her hair. Her disrobing in open court. Her virtue. Her pride. Her ego. Her thirst for revenge. Kurukshetra. The murder of her children. Krishna.

Images of a life lived appeared before the queen.

A vast mountain, a giant peak, dense clouds, a humble abode, two sons, a peaceful, eternal bliss hitherto unknown. The arms of her beloved, his tender touch, his soft lips, his deep mystic eyes. The passion in her, the love that filled her heart so much it could explode, the fire with which she burnt for him, the joy she felt when he was around, the unadulterated satisfaction she sensed at their union, during those innumerable days and nights they spent together ravishing each other with their exuberant flowing dazzle, when time stood still, when he filled her completely because nothing else mattered except their rapt lovemaking.

He, Shiva the God of excess, sometimes the ascetic but usually the sexual and she, Parvati, the transformer.

She knew he had always been there, even when she had forgotten he remembered who she was. Who they truly were what they meant to each other! For they were Shiv and Shakti, the cosmic force that strung all life together. She the *prakriti,* virginal nature and he the *purusha,* the virginal spirit. Without her, his power was nothing, he was nothing for not only did she complement him; she completed him. For without this completion, there would be nothingness, devoid of any shape or any purpose. Theirs was the ultimate, final conjugation that preceded everyone else's yet present in every element of the universe.

Draupadi felt whole. She felt herself. Her True Self. She was his, she always would be, and he belonged to her beyond eternity, beyond the end of all things. He was her true love, her only love, her universal half. Turning to the Lord beside her, a soft smile upon her lips, a coy demeanour in her eyes, her voice awash with love in every fibre of her being she said, "My dear husband…"

Part V

Mother Uma

The goddess who is omnipresent as the personification of universal mother

The goddess who is omnipresent as the embodiment of power

The goddess who is omnipresent as the symbol of peace

Oh Goddess (Devi) who resides everywhere in all living beings as intelligence and beauty,

I bow to her, I bow to her, I bow to her again and again.

—Devi Stuti/Durga Mantra

6

Mahadev looked at Draupadi, his eyes full of tears. She finally knew! She remembered her true form, she remembered him, she remembered who they were to each other. Mahadev's days had been long, this era of separation from his dear wife a burden to bear. He had missed her so much, her boisterous laughter, the way she bit her lower lip when she got nervous, her beautiful skin, those eyes, that luscious body! But, most of all, he missed her steady presence in his life. She was not only his wife but also the person he most depended on for his existence, to keep him going when things got arduous.

Mahadev yearned for her, more than anything else. In this moment, how he wished they could once again intertwine into their most passionate form, embracing their souls and diving ardently into each other. He hoped there were nothing more to do but take her back to their home, where they could be together forever, plunging into their deep ocean of love for eternity. The Great Lord stood mesmerized, abounding with happiness and joy, his eternal source of happiness finally returning to him.

"I have been so unfair to you, my love," the queen began. "But, I did not remember. Will you ever forgive me this huge sin?" Draupadi, her eyes emotional, said to Mahadev. She could not imagine what her husband had been through during her long absence.

"There is nothing to forgive, my darling. Oh, I love you so much it hurts. I am just relieved you have come back to me, that you remember who I am and who we are to each other. Although I knew this day would eventually arrive, I would have paid any price for it to come sooner," the Great Lord said.

"I love you too. I have always loved you. There can never be any other. Let us leave, my love. Let us go home and resume our lives. It has been a long time since I lay in your arms and felt your touch. My worldly duties are now over. I have done everything I was born to do. Let us go back to Kailash and resume our life of bliss."

"How I wish I could carry you away, Gauri," Mahadev said, using the name he always had for her. "Alas, I cannot. For it is not time for Draupadi to leave Earth yet. You must return to Hastinapur and live out the rest of your days with the Pandavas. Once you ascend to heaven, we shall be united never to part again."

Draupadi sighed. She wanted to touch him, caress his soft skin, kiss his full mouth, feel the heat of his body upon hers. Until now, the queen had not realized how much she missed him, how desperately she craved him and how urgently she needed him. But, she knew he was right. He could not touch her yet. Not in this form for she still had to do her duty. Performing it would be the fastest way back to him. For their union, she would have to return to Hastinapur and finish her life in this form, as Maharani Draupadi, wife of the mighty Pandavas. But, before she went back, she knew there was one thing she could do. That alone would hold them both until they reunited.

"I will fulfil my duties to the Pandavas, my dear," she told Mahadev. "However, we must first return to Somnath for I have one final thing to do there."

"What do you have to do there, my love?" the Lord asked her.

"You shall see," Draupadi responded with a smile on her lips.

Maharani Draupadi and the Great Lord returned to Somnath where everything looked the way they had left it. The sturdy temple looked magnificent in the evening sun's rays, its dominant presence casting wide shadows. Summer had given way to autumn with a cool breeze blowing inwardly from the sea through the courtyard lightly swaying the trees and littering fragrant flowers on the ground. Worshippers lined the temple, eager to pay their respects to the *Swayambhu* linga, completely unaware that their earthly vision did not allow them to see the Great Lord and Maharani Draupadi standing right between them. A peaceful calm transcended the entire place similar to what the queen felt in her absolute being.

Draupadi looked at the temple with a newfound reverence. She realized how deeply her journey was linked with Somnath, what her true connection with this magnificent house of worship really was. Climbing up the steps, the queen raced through the temple's main corridor, walking towards the west wall, the Lord trailing behind her. Passing through the central hall into the intermediate corridor, Draupadi touched the giant silver pillars that held the temple's mighty weight, reminiscing about their builder. The queen paused as she came upon the west wall, glaring at the image of the glorious woman who stared back at her. She, from a different era, her image crafted by a man Draupadi thought was pure evil but had come to respect in so many ways. Admiringly, she ran her hands through the face on the wall, tracing the sad eyes that carried illusions of failure and the prim face that held so many burdens. "Oh, the travails you have gone through, Vedavati," the queen spoke quietly to the image.

Draupadi turned to look at the Lord standing behind, her face unable to betray the emotions rising inside. Silently, she walked through the hallway, making her way into the inner sanctum where the queen had started her penance months ago. The Lord walked behind her, quietly curious. He was exhilarated to follow in his wife's footsteps.

Turning to him, Draupadi extended her hand to the Lord. Mahadev looked at her puzzled. "Take it," she said to him.

"Gauri," he began, adoringly, "I cannot touch you yet. As much as I want to, you are not mine in this form. It would not be right."

Draupadi smiled deviously. "Was it right to come into my dreams then and give me pleasures I had not known in this form?"

The Lord smiled, his eyes widening knowing he had been caught. His wife had truly remembered everything, even the dreams he had tried to erase from her memory.

"It was not right, but I could not help myself. I have missed you so much," he replied, longingly. "It has been a long era without you, my love."

"Then take my hand," Draupadi said, slightly impatient.

Hesitatingly, Mahadev extended his hand covering it over the queen's. Draupadi came closer. Her heartbeat quickening, the queen stood directly in front of her husband. Mahadev could feel her breath upon his. He could smell her fragrance; he took a deep breath, closed his eyes, and inhaled her essence. Ah, how he had missed her divine smell! He revelled under his wife's scent, realizing she belonged to him and he to her, that they were always meant to be together, and their union was the guiding principle of this universe. There was no greater truth.

Turning her back to him, still holding his hand, Draupadi led Mahadev around the *Swayambhu* linga, the couple circling it three times. Mahadev walked behind his wife, his eyes shining with his deep love for her, unable to wait for what was to come next. Draupadi walked in front, her heart full of gratitude for this intimate moment the two were able to share.

At the completion of the third circle, Draupadi stopped and turned to the Great Lord.

"Do you know what I just did?" Draupadi asked drawing herself closer to the Lord of all the worlds.

"Yes, I do," Mahadev whispered. "I know very well what you just did," he said embracing his wife, feeling the passion rising through his body, elevated in his soul and spirit. With every fibre of his being, the Great Lord called out her name blissfully relishing her presence, "Uma. My Gauri, my love."

Draupadi melted in her husband's arms, her heart thumping, her soul finally serene. With her divinity firmly in her grasp, the queen clutched her husband's body, welcoming him as he completed their union, the two dissolving into each other's mind, body, and soul.

There, in the inner sanctum, the Lord and Mother Uma completely merged into one while everything in the world disappeared under their orchestra. The ground shook with the intensity of their unity, knowing a great synthesis of energies had taken place, discerning that the primordial force had once again found her spirit. Instantly, a piercing sound rang throughout the entire inner sanctum, vibrating with pulsating energy shaking the earth for several miles, hallowing everything underneath. The two lovers rejoiced in their divine act of creation, while the Earth oscillated in their surroundings, staggering under the tremendous force of Shakti meeting Shiv, beginning emerging from *Shunya* (nothing). Somnath exulted in this spiritual unification that further venerated the temple for all of eternity.

After an aeon, the Lord and the queen sated, released their grip on each other. Embracing her timeless husband once more, Draupadi said, "I must go now. It is time for me to return to my husbands."

Mahadev felt a twang of jealousy knowing he would once again be parted from his wife. The knowledge that she would have to leave created angst in his heart at the pain of separation yet again.

"Why did you circle the *Swayambhu* linga with me, Gauri?" he asked, although aware of the answer.

"You know very well why," the queen said, shyly.

"I do," he said coming close enough to see the rise and fall of Draupadi's chest. "I still want to hear from you," he softly whispered into her ear.

Draupadi's control was slipping yet again. She knew she needed to leave now or else she may never be able to. "My dear husband, I love you beyond all time, but

I must go now." She broke their light embrace and walked away.

Mahadev held her hand as she walked past. "You must say it, Gauri. Otherwise, I am afraid I cannot let you go," he said, playfully.

"Why must you torment me?" Draupadi asked him.

"Unless you have forgotten, that is what I do," Mahadev said, his voice passionate, drawing her closer to him.

Draupadi relented. "I immortalized our union in the past, present, and future, in mind, body, and soul, immanent, transcendent, and absolute. In the presence of the *Swayambhu,* that manifested on its own, I gave myself to you until the *Mahapralaya,* the Great Dissolution and beyond, no matter what form we take and where our earthly allegiances lie."

The Lord kissed her lips tenderly. "Yes, you did and forever you shall be mine."

"I shall come back to you soon, I promise," Draupadi kissed Mahadev back fondly.

"I can wait for you forever," Mahadev replied, tenderly.

Draupadi walked out of the inner sanctum, her entire being radiating with peace as she descended the temple steps leaving Mahadev behind with a magnitude of contentment he had not known in a long time.

He would wait for his wife to return. For without *Shakti* (energy) Shiv would merely remain a *shav* (corpse).

Draupadi retuned to Hastinapur a new queen, with a new perspective. Palace life seemed to continue as it always did, hectic and full of frenzy. Her husbands went about their business of ruling the kingdom, life lingering on as usual. Except nothing was typical for Draupadi anymore. Nothing could remain the same any longer. Her enduring fire was replaced with a yearning for a life so strong that little else mattered. The queen's earthly duties tended to, every waking moment of Draupadi's life was occupied with thoughts of reunification with the Lord of all the worlds; her one and only husband. The queen longed to shed her human form and return to him.

Despite her overpowering wishes, the queen had responsibilities to fulfil, so she threw herself back into daily life. From the moment the rays of the sun hit the land of Hastinapur, the queen tended to her husbands and her royal duties with great fervour, never once giving anyone any reason to doubt her intentions or true wishes. Despite the melancholy, anxiety over separation, and the deep pining over her husband, Draupadi maintained her demeanour as always; poised, dutiful, and graceful. For even though her human form craved freedom, the queen truly understood that performing her duty was the only way to her salvation. Her schedule remained as it always was, busy and full.

Early one morning, on leaving her royal chambers for her regular stroll, Draupadi came upon a forlorn looking Arjuna in the garden.

"O great warrior, why are you here so early and why do you look so sad?" she asked him.

Relief washed over Arjuna seeing his wife. "I was waiting for you, Panchali. Since this is the time of your daily walk in the garden, I decided to wait here for you." According to the arrangement in place since the day the Pandavas wed Draupadi, the queen spent one entire year with each of the brothers during which time no other brother entered her suite. If Draupadi was disturbed by another brother, the brother who erred would need to repent by going into exile for a year. After his exile when he accidentally came upon Draupadi and his eldest brother, Yudhishthira, Arjuna would never make that mistake again. Currently, Nakul resided in her royal chambers.

Draupadi looked upon Arjuna. The best archer in the world looked disturbed, fine lines replacing the youth that once shone on his face. Dark circles sunk his shining brown eyes; grey hair lined his temples. His face, still handsome, was replaced by a battle-weary warrior who prized peace above all else. Arjuna's pride, his glorifying feature, now looked hurt and stung. The mighty Pandava looked vulnerable.

"What is the matter, Arjuna? I have never seen you so downcast before. Your shoulders are droopy, and your body language looks crushed. These are not the features of the Arjuna I know. Is everything all right?" Draupadi asked the man who had won her swayamvara all those years ago.

"I *am* downcast, Panchali. Since Krishna left, nothing has any meaning to it anymore. Life can never be the same for me. I am sure you feel the same way," Arjuna replied.

"Yes, I do feel the same way, Arjuna, but life must still go on. We must do what we are born to do. When those we love, depart, and leave us behind, it hurts and it seems impossible to keep going, but we must," the queen advised her husband.

"But, what does one do when our prime identity is no longer ours, O Draupadi?"

"What do you mean, O great archer?" Draupadi asked puzzled.

"Do not call me that any longer," Arjuna responded, his voice rising with disgust.

"Not call you what? Great archer? But, you are the greatest archer ever born. You are an expert genius of the bow, *Sabyasachi*; the only one in this world who can shoot arrows with both hands. Why can I not call you that? It is who you truly are."

"It is who I used to be, Panchali," Arjuna said, dejectedly. "I can barely shoot arrows with one hand now, leave alone both hands. I do not deserve any epithets that were once conferred on me for I can no longer justify any of them. My skills no longer work, Panchali. Since Krishna left, I have not been the same anymore. I just do not understand why."

"What do you mean your skills no longer work?" the queen questioned, her eyes wide with disbelief.

"They do not, Panchali. I can no longer shoot my arrows; not with half the precision I was able to. I am so confused and do not understand why this is happening."

"But, how is this possible? When did you first notice this, Arjuna?" the queen inquired.

"When I went to Dwarka to bring home those who had survived the incoming ocean. After seeing all the horrors of so many wars, I thought I would be prepared to see Dwarka but the sight that greeted me was unlike anything I have ever seen. So much destruction and just so absolute. The entire city just vanished overnight, Panchali. It was as if nothing ever stood there. The beautiful city of gold that you loved so much was totally gone," Arjuna reminisced.

Draupadi exhaled. Yes, the destruction would be absolute, she thought. "Dwarka met the fate it was supposed to. The city and its inhabitants achieved the purpose they came on Earth to achieve. Their end was brutal, no doubt, but that is what their destiny was."

Arjuna nodded. "On the way back," he continued, "while escorting those who were left behind, we came upon the countryside of Panchanada. Thinking it was a good place to rest, I asked everyone to retire for the day. But, I was mistaken because at night, we were attacked by bandits looking for wealth and women.

I tried, Panchali, I tried to save them," said Arjuna amid sobs, "but nothing worked. My Gandiva was useless, my quiver completely empty. The few arrows I could scrounge, completely missed their mark. So many women died that day because I failed to protect them." Arjuna collapsed grieving on a nearby bench, his head in his hands.

Draupadi walked to her husband. She grieved with him, but she also knew why the women were killed that night. "Do not grieve for those who have died, Arjuna. They have only left behind their earthly bodies; their soul remains safe and intact. Nothing can kill the soul because it is deathless."

Arjuna looked up at Draupadi, stunned at her reply. "You are speaking the words of Krishna, Panchali. Words he spoke to me at Kurukshetra. How do you know them so intimately?"

Draupadi smiled. "I know of the words he spoke to you, Arjuna, for those are the eternal truth. Know, my dear husband, there is no greater truth than the one Krishna disclosed to you on that battlefield. Besides the lesson of law, devotion, and righteous behaviour, the

Bhagavad Gita is the most valuable gift for humankind to emerge from our era and our Lord, Shri Krishna's time on Earth. The words he spoke will be a guiding light for those who wish to follow the path of righteousness, duty, and faith and want to be united with the Supreme Reality.

As far as the women you grieve for who died that day—all 16,100 of them—were apsaras who ardently wished to come to Earth as Krishna's wives. From boons they received, they were able to fulfil their desires and at that moment, when you were with them, it was time for them to depart this world and so they did. So, you see, your grieving for them while extremely admirable is not required," Draupadi explained to Arjuna.

"But, you still did not answer my question, Panchali. How did you know the words our Lord spoke to me? You were nowhere near and Krishna told me never to repeat those words for not everyone would understand. He told me the knowledge was for me alone. And, how do you know about the apsaras and their boons? It seems you are hiding something from me, my queen."

"Do not worry about what I know and why I know it, O great warrior. My knowledge and information are completely irrelevant to our present discourse. I know what I do because it is my responsibility to know. Your job is to focus on your predicament and try to find a suitable solution for it.

So, tell me, Arjuna," Draupadi said, bringing the discussion back to her husband's recent loss of ability. "Is this the only time you noticed that your skills were not working?"

Arjuna shook his head no. "It is not. After he left his earthly form, Krishna came into my dreams and asked me to visit the Sarasvati *Triveni* (confluence) to conduct his final rites. Along with a few villagers, who had also been called by Krishna in their dreams, I completed all his rituals and headed back to Hastinapur. On the way home, I was attacked by goons at night but once again could not defend myself. They beat me up and stole everything from me. I am afraid I can no longer protect myself or anyone else, Panchali. I am a failure. I am so fearful."

Draupadi's heart fluttered at the mention of the Sarasvati *Triveni* and Krishna's final rites. The day was etched in her mind for eternity—the day she found Krishna's body, when she stood upon the Lord's mortal coils, and blessed him. The queen still had Krishna's yellow scarf she found at the river where she had the fortune of seeing Mother Sarasvati and dipping in the Holy *Sangam* (convergence) to attain *moksha* (liberation). Ah, she had come so far!

Draupadi looked at her husband. The once mighty warrior looked lost and defeated. The queen touched her husband's cheek fondly. "You are not a failure, Arjuna; you are a hero, and the world will rightly remember you as such. Just because your skills are not working now, does not erase the fact that they were instrumental throughout your lifetime and helped us win the greatest war against adharma."

"But, that is not what Barbarik said. Do you remember Barbarik?"

"I remember that brave soul Barbarik, the grandson of Bheema and Hidimba, the son of Ghatotkacha. What did he say?" the queen asked puzzled.

"After Krishna gave Barbarik the boon that even if he killed himself, he would retain his power of comprehension and sight, we hoisted his head upon a tree so his final desire of watching the Kurukshetra battle could be fulfilled. At the end of the war, we brothers were playing with each other on who killed the most *adharmis* (godless people). I said it had to be me, Bheema disagreed and said he killed most of the Kuru army. Nakul and Sahadeva each had their own tally of people they had killed, and our eldest brother had his number ready. Unable to come to a consensus, we asked Krishna who amongst us was responsible for most deaths. Krishna then suggested we ask Barbarik resting upon the tree. So, we visited him."

"So, what happened when you visited Barbarik?" Draupadi asked, her pulse quickening.

"It was the most unusual explanation. Barbarik said he saw the most powerful Kuru army standing in their regalia, with their eleven *akshauhinis,* the mighty Bhishma leading the way. He saw Guru Drona, Guru Kripa, Duryodhana, Dushashana, all the other Kauravas ready to fight. He saw Karna's valour and he laid his eyes upon the magnificent Narayani Sena, a sight to behold! Barbarik said he saw the magnificence of the Kuru fighting, their true valour, and their unbinding belief in their cause. He said never had anyone in any of the three *lokas* ever seen an army so massive, so organized, so very commanding." Arjuna paused.

"Okay, and what about our army? What did he say about that?" Draupadi inquired.

"You are not going to believe what he said," Arjuna said nodding his head in utter disbelief. "Barbarik said when he turned towards the Pandava army, he only saw two people. A man and a woman."

Draupadi smiled inwardly. She knew what Barbarik had seen but continued her act.

Exclaiming with disbelief the queen retorted, "Two people? He saw only a man and a woman? There were no women on the battlefield. What about the might of the Pandava army? Did he not see my brave husbands gracing the battlefield or my valiant brothers fighting alongside them? Did he not see our army, our fight for justice? Did he not see any of these things?" she reiterated. "Who did he claim to see anyway?" the queen asked feigning annoyance.

"I agree we had more than two people, we had seven *akshauhinis*, we had mighty warriors, brave souls who laid down their lives for us but that is what Barbarik said he saw."

"So, who did he see?" Draupadi asked again, her voice urgent.

"Barbarik said he saw Lord Krishna annihilating everyone in the Kuru army with his Sudarshan Chakra and..."

"And, who else? Who was the woman he saw?"

"He saw Mother Kali, her tongue spread out drinking the blood of the *adharmis*. I know it is so hard to believe his vision but Barbarik was such a learned soul. What reason would he have to misrepresent anything?"

Draupadi knew Barbarik's vision was accurate for she and Krishna had indeed decimated the entire Kuru army but she continued to act out. "Hard to believe? It is impossible to believe! How can two people replace an entire army? Did Krishna ever corroborate Barbarik's version?" she asked.

"Krishna merely smiled his lopsided grin," Arjuna replied, a smile on his lips in reverence for the friend he had lost. "Never confirmed nor denied it. So, Panchali, tell me was I ever the brave archer of our times then? Or even of Kurukshetra? Who am I? Tell me my identity, Panchali!"

"Arjuna," Draupadi said calmly, "you are and will always remain the greatest archer of all time. Do not despair over what Barbarik saw. The entire world, all dimensions, this universe does and will always hold you the protagonist of the Mahabharata tale. You fought the war courageously, blessed with Krishna by your side as your charioteer. And, do not forget what the Lord promised before the war began—that he would never lift a weapon. Barbarik was a great soul but even great souls can make mistakes. Do not despair over what Barbarik saw. The world will always see you for the hero you are and have always been."

"So, I don't need to worry about losing my power? It could be temporary?" Arjuna asked like a child eager for an answer that would ease his discomfort.

"There must be a reason why the events happened with you. Let me visit Rishi Vyasa's ashram tomorrow. I am sure he will guide us," Draupadi replied.

Arjuna sighed with relief, his insecurities once again smoothed over by his wife. She always knew what to say to make him feel better.

Draupadi, on the other hand, knew why Arjuna was losing his power. She also knew what the Pandavas needed to do next. But, the queen had some loose ends to tie with Rishi Vyasa, so she decided to pay him a visit anyway.

Early the next morning, Draupadi arrived at the sage's ashram. Bowing to the great soul of Sage Vyasa, the queen offered her respects. The learned sage humbled at her presence bowed back deeply.

"Will you not bless me, Sage Vyasa?" the queen asked, humbly.

Sage Vyasa smiled. "Unfortunately, O great queen, I do not have a blessing befitting the primordial shakti of the universe. You are the power behind us all, the mother of all creation. What blessing can I, a modest sage, give you?" Sage Vyasa said, his hands still folded in respect to the queen's divine form.

Draupadi smiled.

"You are not a modest rishi, Sage Vyasa. For it is through you that future generations will learn of what happened in Mahabharata, about the great war of Kurukshetra, about the word of our beloved Lord Krishna, his mighty disciples, the Pandavas, the many injustices they faced and how they fought them persistently. You are the thread that ties us to the future. For your service, we are all in your debt."

"There is no debt incurred when one is performing one's duty, Mother. But, I noticed, you made no mention of yourself. Would the world not learn something from you and your experiences as Maharani Draupadi as well?" Sage Vyasa questioned the queen.

The queen grinned. "Yes, they will. And, I am sure you will do all my experiences justice. However, I wish for you to not write about my divinity. Let us leave only one divine member in this epic tale."

"Why is that, Mother? Should the world not know who you truly are?"

"If the world knows who I truly am they will dismiss all the work I did as divine forbearance. This will mean that men will continue to dismiss women, not take them seriously, not appreciate their resilience and mistake women as trite and trivial. I do not wish for that to happen."

"But, Mother, you know that eventually your fears will come true regardless so why not show the world your amazing power and your selfless sacrifice?"

"You call me a mother and then want to write about my selfless sacrifice? Is it not a mother's nature to indulge in selfless sacrifice? What is so divine or powerful about that, Sage? As far as the rest is concerned, yes, eventually in Kali yuga man will mistreat woman and consider her gender and her strengths a weakness. But, if you tell the truth about me now, it will happen sooner. Besides, not every truth has to be disclosed. Some are just to be left alone. Those who deserve to know, and are worthy, who want to understand the Supreme Reality will identify me and associate me with who I truly am. Those who don't, will continue to live their life blindly."

"I understand, Mother," Sage Vyasa bowed to Draupadi again. "I shall portray all your struggles and strengths but will leave your divinity out. I shall portray you as a great queen who was but a mortal with limitations and faults."

Draupadi agreed. "Yes, please portray me with all my faults for it is only recently that I have learned about my true identity. But, now that I am aware, it would not be correct to cast it on my entire life's journey as Draupadi."

"You are right as always, Divine Mother. I am grateful for your guidance."

"I have one other idea for you, Sage, as you start to compile this great *itihaas*."

"Yes, Mother, tell me."

"Pray to my son, Ganesha, to be your scribe. He loves to write and will do justice to your oral rendition."

"I shall do that, Mother. Shall I tell the world you made this splendid suggestion?" the Sage asked, hoping the queen would acquiesce.

The queen laughed. "You are very persistent, Sage Vyasa. Tell them you prayed to the father of the universe, Lord Brahma who suggested Ganesha write for you."

"As you wish, Mother. I shall do as you say," the rishi replied, dejectedly. His last attempt did not meet with the success he was looking for.

"Now, tell me what else can I do for you," Vyasa continued. "For I sense you are here with another purpose."

Draupadi simpered. "You are perceptive, Sage. There is another matter, it is concerning one of my husbands."

Sage Vyasa looked up at the queen curious.

"Arjuna came to me yesterday," Draupadi continued, "He is beginning to lose his skills. His quiver is empty and the Gandiva is starting to miss its mark. The time for us to depart is drawing close."

"Ah," the sage responded half surprised, half expectant. "Yes, time to depart is indeed coming closer. Normally, I would not recommend anyone undertake the Mahāprasthāna in Kali yuga but..."

"But the demon Kali will not harm the Pandavas since I am with them, Rishi. I will not fall to my death until the Pandavas reach the border of heaven. Kali will dare not go that far and the Pandavas will be safe to conduct the rest of their journey without me, until Yudhishthira ultimately arrives at the gates," the queen interjected.

"No, the demon Kali will dare not touch them with you casting your protective shield around your husbands. Mother, you know all the truths of the world including the one I am about to tell you. But, I would be remiss if I do not mention it."

"Do not hesitate to speak your mind, Sage Vyasa. You know I always value your opinion," Draupadi said.

"I know, Mother, but this is grave. Yet, I shall speak my mind as you command. The Pandavas are growing extremely weak. I have been sensing it for a while now. I fear for them, not their physical safety for you are with them but I am genuinely concerned about their mental state. Very soon, all their other worldly powers will desert them. Sahadeva will no longer continue to be the wisest, Nakul no longer proficient in horses, Arjuna will lose all his archery skills, his Gandiva will soon disappear as his arrows have. Bheema will not have one tenth the strength he used to, and Yudhishthira will slowly lose his dharma as Kali gets powerful on Earth. None of the brothers will be able to bear this. Hence, it is imperative that you undertake this journey as soon as possible.

It is also extremely important that you continue to be incredibly careful as you undertake your final departure. May I suggest that you stay with them a little while longer, until perhaps Yudhishthira reaches the doors of heaven?" the sage asked, earnestly.

"I know why you ask that of me, O great Rishi, but I am afraid I have to disappoint you. For, if I do so, it will go against everything Draupadi is. I must continue to play the part until my final moment on Earth. Only then will everyone be convinced that I was nothing but a mortal queen," the Maharani answered.

Sage Vyasa shook his head. "Such terrible injustice. It is so wrong."

"O great Sage, on my journey with Mahadev, I learnt so many things were so wrong, yet they occurred. I learned about so many acts abiding by dharma, unflinching in their faith, replete with love and devotion that happened but no one ever found out or cared enough to document them properly. Maybe there were other reasons for it, but good people got castigated, called evil even though they were the most learned, the most..." Draupadi looked for words to finish her sentence.

"Human," Rishi Vyasa added.

Draupadi nodded. "Only time and a few fortunate enough to peer through the veil of immense darkness will know their true nature for only a few are worthy. Similarly, only a few will know who I truly was for only a few truly deserve to know it. Not everyone will understand our Lord Krishna's Gita. Same way, not everyone will understand my reality."

"As you wish, Mother," Sage Vyasa bowed to Draupadi.

Draupadi returned to the palace immediately, making her way to see the king, her husband Yudhishthira. Having finished his courtly duties for the day, the queen found the king in his royal apartments.

"My dear husband, how are you today?" the queen asked exchanging pleasantries.

"Panchali, what a sight for sore eyes are you. I was just thinking about you. Wondering when you would return from Rishi Vyasa's ashram."

"Did Arjuna tell you I was visiting Rishi Vyasa?" Draupadi asked.

Yudhishthira nodded. "Yes, he came to me in despair over losing his archery skills. I was very concerned over what he was saying and his state of mind. That is when I suggested he visit you for you always know how to make us all feel better when we are down. He came to me after and told me about your visit.

How did it go at the ashram? What did Rishi Vyasa suggest we do about Arjuna's empty quiver?"

Draupadi sat down on a nearby seat. She would have to break the news gently.

"Yudhishthira," she began her voice calm, "you are a great king. History will remember you as the establisher of dharma (law) upon earth, the truth teller who ruled Hastinapur as was his right."

"I appreciate your kind words, Draupadi, but why don't you come straight to the point? Tell me, what did Rishi Vyasa say?" the king asked.

Draupadi sighed. She decided to do as her husband had suggested. "It is time for us to undertake the Mahāprasthāna, our final journey towards the Himalayas until we all fall and die. All of us have fulfilled the job on Earth we came to do. We have defeated adharma, established a righteous kingdom, and secured a successor. There is no other task left any longer. Arjuna was right, his powers are diminishing. All your powers will diminish and eventually completely leave you. Before that happens, we need to go.

Appoint Parikshit as the next king of Hastinapur, Yudhishthira, and let us make our way north," the queen said with finality.

The dramatic tone of Draupadi's voice and her message made Yudhishthira ill. He had not expected such a final outcome. Yudhishthira had only been ruling for thirty-six years and knew very well the glory he craved would require his reign to last several years more. The king was not yet ready to hand over his kingdom to Parikshit but the thought of him and his brothers losing their powers and deeds scared him. Sage Vyasa would not give such dire advice lightly. Yudhishthira resolved to speak with his brothers before committing to anything.

"Hmm," Yudhishthira began. "I hear you, Panchali, but I cannot take a decision of this magnitude on my own. Why don't all of us get together this evening so everyone has a chance to express their opinion?"

"As you wish," the queen responded.

That evening, after dinner, Yudhishthira asked his brothers and Draupadi to meet him in his royal apartments where he laid before them the dilemma that confronted them. He also told them of Draupadi's visit to Rishi Vyasa and the sage's advice to the brothers and their queen.

The brothers sat still with the knowledge of losing their powers. No one wanted to leave but being less than on Earth was not acceptable either. Uncomfortable as they were, the Pandavas decided to follow Sage Vyasa's advice. They, along with Draupadi, would undertake the Mahāprasthāna. But first, Parikshit needed to be crowned king.

Thus, it was decided that on the auspicious day of Ram Navami, the ninth day of Chaitra, Parikshit, son of Uttara and Abhimanyu, grandson of Subhadra and Arjuna, would be crowned king of Hastinapur. The dynasty of the Kuru kingdom would pass from King Yudhishthira to the next generation. In preparation for taking over, Yudhishthira imparted several lessons on dharma, whereas Parikshit's grand uncles, Bheema, Nakul, and Sahadeva and his grandfather taught him the art of warfare and strategy.

On the anointed day, Sage Vyasa placed the heavy crown on the young king's head amid great fanfare. The kingdom, although sad knowing the Pandavas intended to give up their earthly forms, rejoiced at the new king and his queen, Madravati.

For Draupadi, this moment held special significance; both bitter and sweet. Passing the torch to the future enabled her and her husbands to meet their fate but her human heart stung with the realization that it was not Prativindhya, her son with Yudhishthira, the eldest Upapandava, sitting atop that throne. Even still, she celebrated this moment with all the love in her heart, blessing the new rulers with great success and prosperity.

Parikshit and Madravati would be good rulers and although the new king would meet an undeserving end, he would leave behind a great legacy in the form of his eldest son, Janamejaya. Emperor Janamejaya, the first human ever to hear the *Mahabharata* as written by Sage Vyasa and narrated by his pupil, Vaishampayana. Emperor Janamejaya, the ruler who would be responsible for retelling and spreading the word of the *Mahabharata,* the epic tale of his family's fight against adharma throughout the land. And that, for Draupadi meant everything.

Finally, the day of the Mahāprasthāna dawned. Leaving the palace, their material belongings and all their worldly attachments behind, the five Pandavas and their queen Draupadi started their northward walk to climb the great Himalayas, towards their ultimate destination, Mount Sumeru.

The journey was arduous, the distance long. Draupadi knew she had to hold on until her entourage reached the border of heaven, where Kali could no longer harm her defenceless husbands. She looked at them, one last time in their human form, knowing their fate all too well. These five men with whom the queen had spent so many years, often in so much turmoil, nonetheless remained dear to her. These five men, despite all their faults, cherished their queen, tried to abide by her wishes and tried to give her all the happiness they had promised. In these final moments, Draupadi felt emotional and for the first time ever, the queen kissed each of her husbands in the other's presence; a testament to her impartiality towards them, her farewell to these brave men.

As the queen and the Pandavas kept walking, Draupadi dithered with the decision to give herself up. If she did, her husbands would be defenceless for the remainder of the journey to Kali's temptations. If she did not, they would know her true nature. Deciding to stick to her original plan, the queen fell on the hard, icy ground, her body unable to go any further, her right palm extended out calling each of her husbands by name. While none of them turned back, Draupadi successfully cast a beam of protection around each of her husbands, making them further secure against any malfeasance Kali could attempt. Her ultimate task done, this queen, the brave and mighty Draupadi, princess of Panchal, incarnate of Mother Kali, the strongest woman of all time, breathed her last. Amidst the snow-capped Himalayan peaks, Maharani Draupadi of Hastinapur, wife of the Pandavas, the *Shakti* (energy) of the universe ascended to the heavens.

Her being felt light as she rose through the clouds, arriving at the gates of heaven. So, this is what it felt like to shed your human body, she thought. There were no cares, there were no emotions. None of it mattered any longer. Draupadi was gone, what was important to her was left behind on Earth. Every feeling in her body was replaced by an intense vibration, the energy humming through her palpably.

Surrounded by heavy fog, she felt a shadowy presence behind her. As she turned, she noticed glimpses of figures walking towards her through the dense clouds. Perceptively, she knew who had come to welcome her. She waited as the figures materialized, inhaling their divine fragrance, leaving no doubt in her mind of their identity.

Resplendent in their heavenly forms, Mahadev and Vishnu stood before her welcoming her home, their eyes glittering with joy, their faces shining with a smile.

"We have awaited your arrival anxiously," Vishnu said. "For without you, *Shakti,* nothing in this universe is complete. Now that you have shed your human form, everything can be whole again."

Mahadev stepped forward to her. "Gauri, my love, you have finally returned to me. Let us go home now," he said, embracing her with longing.

She smiled. She had looked forward to this moment for so long. She was ready.

"Not yet, Mahadev," Vishnu interjected. "She cannot leave yet. Her task is yet unfulfilled."

"What more will you have me do, Vishnu?" Uma asked, a grin forming on her face.

Stepping closer to her, Vishnu kissed her hands. "Uma, my sister, you are the dearest to me. How I longed to see you in this form, whole again. My heart rejoices knowing you have returned to us. But, before you leave with Mahadev to your abode in Mount Kailash, there are a few things we need to conclude."

"Like what? What remains unfulfilled now?" Uma asked, innocently.

"Like what is your connection with Ravana. I am sure you remember how I refused to answer that question at the end of Vedavati's life," Mahadev said.

"I do remember, husband. I remember quite clearly how you first brought it up and then dismissed it," Uma replied grinning.

"I did not respond to you, Gauri, for I did not think I was the right person to do so. Now, the right person is in our midst, and I am sure he will be happy to respond," said Mahadev turning to Vishnu.

Vishnu smiled his askew smirk. "Why are you involving me, Mahadev? The conversation was between the two of you. Why don't you finish it as well?" Vishnu joked with them.

"I cannot finish a conversation I was not a part of," Mahadev replied. "Gauri's connection to Ravana must be divulged by you. For you were there and you were partly responsible for what happened. If you do not say it, everyone will assume the incorrect version."

"Which incorrect version?" Uma asked.

"The version of what really happened at Draupadi's disrobing in Hastinapur that fateful day," Vishnu replied with remorse rising in his tone.

"What is incorrect about the events that occurred that terrible day and what does it have to do with Ravana?" Uma asked.

"O Mother of the universe, nothing is hidden from you. You are our ultimate beginning and the eventual end. Without your *Shakti* no thought can be born, nor can it germinate. You know the truth of us all, including the truth of Ravana and of his deep connection to Draupadi."

Uma paused as the realization dawned on her. Her gaze transfixed at Vishnu, she spoke, "Yes, I know now. I know of the deep connection between the two."

"Speak it, Gauri," Mahadev said. "Speak it for if you do not, it will not take form."

"Krishna never helped Draupadi at the disrobing," Uma began, her gaze once again on Vishnu.

Vishnu nodded no. "No, he did not," he added.

"Krishna merely called out to Draupadi's good deeds throughout her lifetimes and asked them to come to her aid in her dire moment of need. It was Draupadi all along who helped herself. It was Draupadi's penance as Vedavati, her deeds as Chaya, her meditation as Nalayani that rescued her that day in Hastinapur. It was on Ravana's suggestion that Vedavati did not curse him, thus saving her intense energies for use another time. Had Ravana not advised that she do so and instead become the cause of his death in another life, Draupadi may not have been able to save herself during her disrobing in that court. For Vedavati's intense penance led the way to Draupadi's rescue."

Vishnu and Shiva nodded in acknowledgment. Uma had spoken.

"Yes, it was Draupadi and her deeds the entire time. It was she who saved herself in the court that day from Dushashana, it was she who entered the battlefield at Kurukshetra to destroy evil, it was she who saved her husbands from Kali as they began their final journey. It was you, my sister, mother of this universe in Draupadi's form," Vishnu added. "You were the glue who bound them together, the energy that gave them strength. It was you who gave them their proficiency, who kept them adroit. Without you, the Pandavas were nothing."

"Were?" Uma asked. "Do you mean they have all fallen to their death now and reached heaven?"

"They have," Mahadev interjected. "It is time for you to meet them one last time. Let us go."

Uma, Mahadev, and Vishnu made their way to *Swarga Loka*, towards the beautiful and grand city of Lord Indra, Amaravati, abiding with unimaginable beauty and riches, fragrant and everlasting gardens, fulfilment of every wish, material or otherwise. Divine apsaras (angels) imparting spiritual knowledge through their art stood well attended by numerous folks who had the fortune to be granted access to this special place.

The three travelled through the gates and the city streets, holding everyone who was blessed to see them in great awe, finally arriving at the palace of Lord Indra. There the King of the Gods was holding court, welcoming his guests from Earth; lucky souls who had reached this plane by leading righteous earthly lives.

Upon seeing them arrive, Lord Indra immediately vacated his throne and bowed to the divinity who bestowed blessings on him.

"It is an honour to see all of you here today," Lord Indra addressed the divine three before him.

"We are pleased to be here," Mahadev responded, "But, we are here for a special reason," he added.

Indra bowed to the Lord of all the worlds. He knew why they were here. "Yes, my Lord Mahadev. I am aware of your reason," he replied glancing at his wife, Uma. "Mother Uma, your humble servant offers you his respects," he said.

"Bless you, Lord Indra. I bless you with prosperity and fair judgement. Never will you waiver in your work and endless shall be your mercy to those who are deserving."

Indra bowed gratefully then continued. "Speaking of deserving," he said. "The Pandavas have all reached here safely. I shall take you to see them. Just a word of caution, Yudhishthira arrived here only moments ago, and they all have only momentarily been reunited. They may still be disoriented.

Mother," Indra said continuing to address Uma, "they were all heartbroken to not find you here."

Uma smiled. They would soon find her.

Lord Indra led the three to where the Pandavas were situated. Noisy and boisterous, the brothers were overjoyed to find each other again and unite with their eldest brother, Karna.

Vishnu, Mahadev, and Uma walked into their presence followed the King of the Gods. Recognizing Vishnu and Mahadev instantly, the men fell to the Gods' feet prostrating themselves. Vishnu and Mahadev blessed them.

Karna was the first to speak. "My Lords, seeing you here makes all my life's struggles worthwhile. But, pray tell us, O Lords, who is this stunning lady with you who shines brighter than all the stars in the universe?"

Uma looked at Karna, the man Draupadi had once loved then had come to hate. Her eyes flitted from his face to the face of the Pandavas, each of Draupadi's five husbands. No one's face lit up with any flicker of recognition.

Vishnu laughed. "This woman," he said pointing to Uma, "she is Mother Uma, Mahadev's wife," he said to immediate offers of respect from the men.

"Forgive me, O Mother, for not recognizing you," Karna said.

"You have still not recognized me, O Karna," Uma added. "For I am now Uma but all of you know me by a different name."

The men looked worried. "What name, O Mother?" Yudhishthira asked his hands folded.

"I am surprised you of all people have not yet recognized her, Yudhishthira," Mahadev spoke. "This woman who is my wife, the love of my existence, my Gauri once used to be your wife."

"My wife?" Yudhishthira asked baffled. "How can Mother Uma ever have been my wife, O Lord?"

"She was your wife, Yudhishthira. You just did not know who she truly was," Mahadev turned to the

Pandavas. "She was once all of your wife. She belonged to each one of you, and all of you loved her with all your heart even though you were repeatedly burnt with the intensity of her flames."

Recognition dawned in Yudhishthira's eyes. "My Lord, do you mean Mother Uma was Draupadi?" he said the words slowly and softly. His brothers looked at him as if he had completely lost his senses.

"Yes, I was Draupadi," Uma confirmed. "I was the princess of Panchal, the wife of the mighty Pandavas, queen of Hastinapur, Maharani Draupadi."

The brothers, aghast at the knowledge of her true nature, fell to her feet. "Mother, forgive us our sins, forgive us all our bad deeds. If we ever said something that was harsh to you as our wife, forgive us," they spoke in terrified unison.

Uma laughed. "There is nothing to forgive, O Pandavas. You are all brave souls, who performed your part valiantly on Earth. Your actions were towards your wife, Draupadi, not me. As husbands, although sometimes you frustrated her, you always performed your dharma. For that, I will forever be pleased with you."

"Mother, I am in special need of forgiveness for I sat by and let Duryodhana and Dushashana assault you in court that day. I do not know what happened to me but that day this Karna became less of a man for not standing up to protect a woman," Karna said, his eyes teary, his hands folded.

Uma turned to him. "Sometimes good people do bad things. What you did that day in court was reprehensible, but it does not make you a bad person nor does it wash away all your other good deeds. You were a great warrior, a generous man, and a faithful friend to Duryodhana. History will remember you as such," the goddess replied.

"Mother, your mercy is endless," Karna said, bowing with great humility.

"Mother," Yudhishthira spoke. "There was an incident that had bothered me for a long time, but I was too afraid to ask anyone for fear of being ridiculed. But now, seeing you here today, confirms all my suspicions."

"Speak, Yudhishthira. Tell us what is on your mind." Uma replied.

"One night when I was in your chambers, spending the year with you, I woke up to a noise. When I opened my eyes, I thought I saw the entire room filled with people of all ages. Men, women, children, young and old, sick and healthy, all lined up by the bed to touch Draupadi's feet. Fear and dread filled my heart for I could not imagine if I was truly awake or dreaming. How can so many people be in our home, in our room at night?

I could never explain this, nor I understood why they were offering their respects to Draupadi. Tell me, that experience was real, Mother. Please tell me it had something to do with you," Yudhishthira beseeched.

Vishnu chuckled.

"It had everything to do with her," he responded to Yudhishthira. "Those were the souls who knew Draupadi's true identity, an incarnate of Mother Kali, the primordial Kundalini, Nirgun, Shakti of this universe, the destroyer of injustice. All of them came to your palace that night and many other nights, visited Draupadi throughout her life, to seek blessings from this incredible goddess who had decided to be born on Earth as your wife and lead you brothers on the path of dharma. For without her guidance, none of you would amount to anything.

She gave you strength at a supernatural level, she gave you the energy to keep you progressing, she counselled you in your times of need, she became your spark in times of injustice and most of all she protected you when you were weak. Without her, the Pandavas would have not been able to fulfil their true potential. For without her, history would not remember you brothers, even you Karna, with the same glory.

She will forever be etched on Earth as Maharani Draupadi, the only woman in the history of humankind, to ever marry the five greatest warriors of all time and you together forever shall be known as her husbands. Your identity shall forever be tied to hers, for without her presence none of this would have been possible. Without her the war of Kurukshetra could not ever have been won," Vishnu said, divulging Uma's true essence to the brothers who listened in rapt amazement.

"Mother," Arjuna stepped forward, his hands in prayer position. "We owe you our lives, our existence, all our victories, but most of all we owe you the establishment of dharma. Without your blessing we would not have won the greatest war of all time. We give you all our souls as an offering for your immense grace upon us."

"Arjuna, there is no need for you to give me anything in return. My actions were simply a result of my duty to fight for what is right. Vishnu fought the same fight alongside you. I was honoured to be a part of it.

My life as Draupadi fraught with injustice was meant to serve as an example for what not to do with women. All women are divine, for they are creators. As such, it is imperative for society to hold them in high regard, respect them and never ill-treat them. What happened to Draupadi, although will become common in Kali yuga, was meant as a lesson for humankind to understand that injustice, especially against women, never wins.

So, understand this, Arjuna, while your life had a purpose, as did my earthly form. And, now that I have shed it, I am eager to return to my home," the goddess said.

"Where shall you go, Mother?" Nakul asked.

"My wife will come with me to our home on Mount Kailash," Mahadev replied.

"Yes," Uma said. "It is time for Shiv and Shakti to be reunited, it is time for the union of the energies once more. For without it, the universe becomes susceptible to weakness. My time here is finished."

Uma cast one final look at the Pandavas and Karna. She then embraced her brother, Vishnu, bidding him goodbye for now. He would return to Vaikuntha.

Leaving the Pandavas behind in *Swarga Loka,* Uma and Mahadev walked out to finally begin their journey to Mount Kailash.

At long last, Uma was heading home.

There are thousands of occasions for joy and hundreds of occasions for fear;

These affect only him that is ignorant but never him that is wise;

With uplifted arms I am crying aloud but nobody hears me.

From Righteousness comes Wealth, also Pleasure;

Why should not Righteousness, therefore, be courted?

For the sake neither of pleasure, nor of fear, nor of cupidity should anyone cast off Righteousness.

Indeed, for the sake of even life one should not cast off Righteousness;

Righteousness is eternal. Pleasure and Pain are not eternal;

Jiva is eternal. A body is not so.

—Svargarohana Parva,
Mahabharata Book 18, Chapter 5

Author's Note

This is a work of fiction. I have always been fascinated with the character of Draupadi and how she was portrayed as just another queen. It has always puzzled me why there was no talk of her divinity because in my mind there is no question, she was divine. As I say in the story, how is it possible for a woman married to the five greatest warriors of all time, to be ordinary? Throughout the *Mahabharata,* hardly anyone has mentioned the divinity aspect of this great queen although there have been many clues for those of us paying attention.

The idea for this story came to me in the aftermath of the 2020 elections in the United States. I had just come out of a gruelling battle for State Senate in New Jersey and despite all my hard work, lost the race. As I lay nursing my wounds, I thought of all great women—real and fiction—and instantly my mind started to revolve around Draupadi, who I have admired since I was a little girl. I have read the *Mahabharata* countless times, starting at a very young age, and each time the story teaches me something new. In my humble opinion, it is the best book ever written with innumerable nuances within each character. As great as the story is, though, I feel it does tremendous disservice to Draupadi casting her mainly as someone who constantly nagged her husbands for the injustice meted out to her, relegated to a sideshow in her husbands' lives.

Truth be told, Draupadi was so much more than an aggrieved woman seeking justice at the hands of those who had wronged her repeatedly. She held the five brothers together, understood their dispositions, and adopted to five very different and sometimes, difficult personalities. One may question my use of the word difficult for the Pandavas, but how can five men at the top of their profession, constantly seeking glory, involved in the worst war ever not have their own egos and frustrations? Even though they were children of god, they were humans and as such, subject to the limitations we all face, although maybe not in the same magnitude. To manage and please them would be no small task.

Draupadi played a pivotal role in the life of the Pandavas. Despite being born fully grown and having no childhood; consequently, very little experience with parents growing up, she nurtured her five husbands, supported them, and made them the best versions of themselves. The saying goes: *behind every successful man is a woman*. Nowhere is this truer than in the case of the Pandavas and their wife, Draupadi.

Although she was a remarkable woman and a great queen, Draupadi has often been misunderstood and misjudged, blamed for events that were not her fault. It could not be further from the truth that she was the cause of the Kurukshetra War. The Great War was a result of Dhritarashtra's lasting greed and his son, Durodhyana's ego. Draupadi was Krishna's closest friend and ally; their relationship was mutually reciprocated. Therefore, it seems baffling to me that someone so close to him would push her husbands towards bloodshed when Krishna was looking for a peaceful solution. Draupadi was also a kind woman as evidenced when she did not pass the death sentence on Ashwatthama who murdered her five sons, although she had every right. If a woman forgave the man who killed her sons in cold blood, would she push her husbands towards countless deaths to avenge her insults?

These baseless insinuations against her character are pathetic and the futile attempt of those wanting to disparage strong women who are not afraid to use their voice. By calling her names and holding her responsible for the actions of men, these narratives are keeping patriarchy alive and well.

Draupadi was a majestic woman and an impressive queen who personally experienced the harsh realities women experience everyday today. There are rarely, if any, instances of royal women treated the way Draupadi was but nevertheless she survived everything thrown at her. She is a beacon of hope for women fighting against injustice and for those working to establish equality in society. It may take a long time but, in the end, truth always wins. If nothing else, I have tried to portray that simple caveat with this tale.

I hope I managed to do an iota of justice to this Goddess.

Rupande Mehta

Appendix

Part I: Draupadi

- Krishna: Hindu deity. Eighth incarnation of Vishnu. Supreme God
- Dwarka: Krishna's ancient city of gold
- Kalki: Vishnu's tenth avatar on Earth
- Demon Kali: Reigning lord of the last yuga, Kali yuga
- Jyotirlinga: A shrine where Lord Shiva is worshipped in the form of a Linga (pillar) of light
- Gandhari: Wife of Dhritarashtra, mother of one hundred Kaurava sons and one daughter
- Dhritarashtra: Blind king of Hastinapur, brother of King Pandu, father of one hundred Kaurava sons and one daughter
- Kauravas: Descendants of the Kuru clan, usually used to denote the one hundred sons of Dhritarashtra and Gandhari
- Pandavas: Five sons of King Pandu of Hastinapur married to Draupadi
- Barbarik: Son of Ghatotkacha and Maurvi. Grandson of Hidimba and Bheema
- Bheema: Second eldest brother of the five Pandavas, possessed superhuman strength. Draupadi's husband

- Yudhishthira: Eldest of the Pandavas. King of Hastinapur. Draupadi's husband
- Dushashana: Kaurava, tried to disrobe Draupadi in open court
- Kurukshetra: City where the Great War is believed to have taken place
- Agni: Fire
- Badabagni: An inextinguishable flame born from Lord Shiva's third eye and carried underwater by the river Sarasvati to protect humankind
- Maharani: Great queen
- Sudarshan Chakra: Spinning discus; weapon belonging to Vishnu
- Arjuna: Third of the five Pandava brothers, greatest archer of all time. Draupadi's husband
- Vaikuntha: Heavenly abode of Goddess Lakshmi and Lord Vishnu
- Ashwatthama: Warrior at Kurukshetra, killer of Draupadi's five sons, son of Dronacharya
- Mother Kali: Primordial Hindu Goddess. Another aspect of Mother Parvati, wife of Lord Shiva
- Shiva: Destructor of the universe. Part of the Holy Trinity along with Brahma and Vishnu
- Mahadev: Greatest God, one of Shiva's 108 names
- Neelkanth: The Blue-throated one, one of Shiva's 108 names
- Pashupatinath: Lord of all living beings, one of Shiva's 108 names
- Gangadhara: Lord of the River Ganga, another name for Lord Shiva

- Vedas: Holy scriptures containing hymns, philosophy, and guidance on the early Vedic religion. Rig Veda, Sama Veda, Yajur Veda, and Atharva Veda
- Satya yuga: The age of truth/golden age, when humanity is governed by gods, and every manifestation is close to the purest ideal and humanity will allow intrinsic goodness to rule supreme. Satya yuga lasts 1,728,000 human years or 4,800 divine years
- Treta yuga: Second of the four yugas (world ages) in a yuga cycle. It lasts 3,600 divine years, or 1,296,000 human years
- Dwapara yuga: The third of the four yugas in a yuga cycle. According to the Puranas, this yuga ended when Krishna returned to his eternal abode of Vaikuntha. Dwapara yuga lasts 864,000 years or 2,400 divine years
- Kali yuga: The fourth and worst of the four yugas in a yuga cycle, followed by the next cycle's Satya yuga. It is the present age, which is full of conflict and sin. According to Hinduism, Kali yuga began 5,122 years ago and as of 2021 has 426,878 years left. Kali yuga will end in the year 428,899 CE
- Shiv Shambhu: The auspicious one, one of Shiva's 108 names
- Yajnaseni: One who emerged from the fire. Another name for Draupadi

Part II: Vedavati

- Vishnu: Preserver and protector of the universe. Part of the Holy Trinity along with Brahma and Mahesh (Shiva)

- Brahma: Creator of the universe. Part of the Holy Trinity along with Vishnu and Mahesh (Shiva)
- Shvetavaraha: Fifty years of Brahma are supposed to have elapsed, and we are now in the Shveta-Varaha Kalpa or the first day of his fifty-first year. According to the Matsya Purana, there are 30 kalpas in all
- Kalpa: Aeon
- Ashwamedha yagna: A horse sacrifice ritual performed by kings to prove their imperial sovereignty
- Srauta: Anything based on the Vedas
- Maharaj: Great king
- Maharishi: A great sage
- Gārhapatya: Belonging to the master/mistress of the house. Here, used to denote the fire belonging to Goddess Durga
- Rama: The seventh incarnation of Vishnu, Sita's husband
- Choghadiya Muhurat: A specific time in the Hindu calendar
- Kartika: Month from the Hindu calendar
- Devadasis: Female dancers and courtesans in a Hindu temple
- Dasyus: Aboriginal people of India
- Puranas: Hindu religious texts
- Pind daan: Ritual performed to bring peace and salvation to the departed souls of ancestors
- Kusha grass: Halfa grass, Big Cordgrass, and Salt reed grass. Scientifically known as *Desmostachya bipinnata*

- Moksha: Liberation from the cycle of birth and death
- Devi Sati: Lord Shiva's first wife. She immolated herself when her father insulted her and her husband, Shiva
- Dakshayani: Another name for Devi Sati, first wife of Lord Shiva
- Sage Narada: God-sage, a travelling musician and storyteller, who carries news, sometimes gossip, and enlightening wisdom
- Sage Shukracharya: Son of Bhrigu, learned sage, teacher of the demons
- Ravana: Ten-headed demon king of Lanka, kidnapped Sita, killed by Rama
- Maha-Brahman: Extremely learned individual
- Veena: A chordophone musical instrument
- Bhishma: Granduncle of the Kauravas and the Pandavas. First commander of the Kuru army at Kurukshetra
- Dronacharya: Teacher of the Kauravas and the Pandavas
- Karna: Kunti's (mother of the Pandavas) first born. Durodhyana's friend, commander of the Kuru army at Kurukshetra

Part III: Chaya

- Ayodhya: Birthplace of Rama, the seventh incarnation of Vishnu
- Hanuman: Hindu god and divine monkey companion of Rama

- Yojana: Unit of measurement in ancient India. 1 yojana = 8 miles/13 kms
- Gopī-jana-vallabha: Lover of the cowherd maidens of Vraja, a region on both sides of the Yamuna river. Another name for Krishna
- Hiranyakashipu: Demon son of Diti and Kashyapa, brother of Hiranyaksha
- Hiranyaksha: Demon son of Diti and Kashyapa who attempted to destroy Earth goddess
- Dantavakra: King of Karusha
- Shishupala: King of Chedi, cousin of Krishna
- Rajasuya yagna: Vedic ritual of the consecration of a king
- King Dasharatha: King of Ayodhya, father of Rama, Bharat, Lakshmana, and Shatrughna
- Kausalya: Wife of King Dasharatha, mother of Lord Rama, eldest queen of Ayodhya
- Sumitra: Wife of King Dasharatha, mother of twins Lakshmana and Shatrughna, second consort and queen of Ayodhya
- Kaikeyi: Wife of King Dasharatha, mother of Bharata, third consort and queen of Ayodhya
- Saptarishi Vasishtha: One of the seven great sages of India, chief author of Mandala 7 of the Rigveda
- Ikshvaku: First king of the Ikshvaku dynasty
- Putrakameshti yagna: Special ritual performed in Hinduism to have a son
- Shukla Paksha: Period of 15 days, which begins on the New Moon day and culminates on the Full Moon

day. Considered auspicious because it is favourable to growth or expansion on every plane of existence that is mental, physical, and spiritual plane

- Chaitra: Month in the Hindu calendar
- Kaamya karma: Ritual with specific objective
- Purusha Suktam: Hymn 10.90 of the Rigveda, dedicated to the Purusha, the Cosmic Being, that is, Vishnu
- King Janaka: King of Mithila, father of Sita
- Swayamvara: Ritual in ancient India where a woman gets to choose a husband from a group of suitors
- Pinaka: Lord Shiva's bow
- Tridev: Holy Trinity of Brahma, Vishnu, and Shiva
- Tridevi: Sarasvati, Lakshmi, and Parvati; the female counterparts of the Tridev
- Shambara: Demon in the Bhagavata Purana, one of Hinduism's eighteen great Puranas
- Manthara: Family servant of Kaikeyi
- Gurukul: Type of education system in ancient India where students live with the teacher/guru at his ashram
- Chitrakoot: Forest where Rama, Sita, and Lakshmana spent eleven years and six months of their fourteen years of banishment
- Sage Valmiki: Author of *Ramayana,* the epic tale of Rama and Sita
- Kulguru: Teacher of the clan
- Saptarishi Agastya: One of the seven great sages of India

- Kalkeya: Powerful, ferocious, and cruel clan of the demons
- Mandodari: Ravana's wife
- Ashoka Vatika: Garden in Lanka where Sita was held
- Keshav: Another name for Lord Krishna

Part IV: Nalayani

- King Drupada: Ruler of Panchala, Draupadi's father
- Prishati: Queen of Panchala, Drupada's wife, Draupadi's mother
- Dhrishtadyumna, Shikhandi, Satyajit: Draupadi's brothers
- Kamsa: Evil ruler of Mathura, Krishna's uncle
- Sahadeva and Nakul: Twins, youngest Pandava brothers, Draupadi's husbands
- Nala and Damayanti: Rulers of Nishadha
- Ardhanarishvara: Is a composite form of Shiva and Parvati depicted as half-male and half-female, equally split down the middle
- Satva, Rajas, Tamas: Three qualities in Hindu philosophy present in all living things in the world. Satva means goodness, calmness, harmonious; rajas for passion, activity, movement; and tamas for ignorance, inertia, laziness

Part V: Mother Uma

- Panchali: Another name for Draupadi
- Gandiva: Arjuna's divine bow made by Brahma

- Bhagavad Gita: One of the most important scriptures of Hinduism. Narrated to Arjuna by Krishna before the start of the Great War
- Akshauhini: Described in the *Mahabharata* as a battle formation consisting of 21,870 chariots, 21,870 elephants, 65,610 horses, and 109,350 infantry men. Each *akshauhini* consisted of 218,700 warriors
- Narayani Sena: Army of Krishna which he used to build his kingdom and safeguard it from others. It fought against the Pandavas at Kurukshetra
- Sage Vyasa: Author of *Mahabharata* and compiler of the Vedas
- Ganesha: Parvati's son, remover of obstacles, elephant-headed God
- Mahāprasthāna: The great or final departure. It means walking continuously towards the north, the Himalayan mountains, without food and rest, until the body falls and dies out of sheer exhaustion
- Parikshit: King of Hastinapur after Yudhishthira, grandson of Subhadra and Arjuna
- Ram Navami: The day of Lord Rama's birth
- Upapandavas: Pandavas' sons with Draupadi
- Madravati: Parikshit's wife, queen of Hastinapur after Draupadi
- Janamejaya: Parikshit's son. Next ruler of Hastinapur
- Vaishampayana: Sage Vyasa's pupil
- Mount Sumeru: Sacred five-peaked mountain of Hindu, Jain, and Buddhist cosmology. Considered to

be the centre of all the physical, metaphysical, and spiritual universes

- Mount Kailash: Heavenly abode of Parvati and Shiva
- Lord Indra: King of the Gods

Acknowledgments

Writing is a solitary exercise, but publishing is not. *Trihayani—The Untold Story of Draupadi* holds a special place in my heart not only because it is my first book but also an amalgamation of many ideas that I have held for the better part of my life. It has been a blessing to bring this vision to reality in which many have partaken.

My grandma, Baji, who instilled in me a love of writing and storytelling is where all of this began. To her, I owe everything. If she were alive, she would merely repeat what she always told me, "Write. Just write, for it is your destiny." Baji, I finally took your advice. I am sure she is smiling in heaven.

Baji's youngest daughter, Chichi, has always been more a friend and less an aunt. I thank her for her patient, long hours on the phone from India discussing every aspect of this story as it was being written, thinking through every nuance and untiringly reading and re-reading it several times. I thank her for the unabashed encouragement and support, for believing in me and knowing that someday this book would be born.

My brother, Jagrut, for recommending the title, effortlessly capturing the entire essence of the story in one single word. My friends, without whom I would be so much less, Kirthi and Sharda. Every woman should have such blazing, loving, caring, and unconditional friends in their corner; in whose eyes you could do no wrong. I thank them for listening to my ideas, offering suggestions, and reading every chapter as it was written. Their energy is so mightily infectious and positive, and I am blessed to have them in my life.

My mother-in-law, Claudette, a woman who has always stood by me and told me I can do whatever I set my mind to; even when I did not believe I could. The universe is very kind to me in allowing me so many precious moments with her in this lifetime.

My publisher Dipankar Mukherjee, editor Indrani Ganguly, and the team at Readomania for seeing the potential of this story and jumping on it when many others did not have the tenacity to. I thank them for their vision and their work in helping me bring *Trihayani* to this world.

The couplet, quoted in Nalayani's chapter, "You are Prakṛti, and I Purusha..." is translated by Stella Kramrisch. Thank you, Stella.

To you, the reader who picked up *Trihayani* and took the time to read it...I hope the story gave you what you needed.

Lastly, the two people for whom I live and for whom every single action of my life is based on. My husband Andrew who makes every day beautiful to live and my entire existence, my daughter Sophie without whom I would still be wandering the hollow emptiness of my mind. Thank you for your patience, your love and for always pushing me to do better. I am so honoured you both chose me. *I love you so much!*

Rupande Mehta

New Jersey, 2022

About the Author

Born in India, Rupande immigrated to the United States in 2002 for her Master's. Currently, she is a professional working for a Fortune 500 company and an activist for causes related to violence against women, environment, and social justice. In 2020, Rupande ran for state level office receiving the most votes ever received by a Democrat for that seat. *Trihayani* is Rupande's first novel. She lives in New Jersey with her husband and daughter. Rupande can be found on Twitter @rupandemehta.

Readomania

Readomania exists to nurture, curate, and bring to you content you love. We are a publishing house that takes pride in encouraging talent, new or old, and provide a wonderful platform for awesome stories.

We make this possible in multiple ways.

The first as an independent publishing house. Readomania boasts of multiple imprints across various categories—fiction, nonfiction, children, to name a few. An eclectic mix of content for its readers, when you read a Readomania title, you enter a world that's yours, supported by unique and quality narratives.

The second, as an online publishing platform for writers—a place to share stories, poems, opinions, travelogues, a way to explore your creative talent. Available as premium, as well as free-to-read content across multiple genres, the reader is spoilt for choice.

Join us in this journey, as we explore, develop, and present stories to our readers and audiences. Welcome to the world of Readomania, get ready to craft stories that enrich lives.

You can visit us at: www.readomania.com